TV FUTURE

A Novella of the Dystopian Future

Lance Horsman

Yamabushi Publishing

This story was born from a quote attributed to one of the greatest Science fiction Authors of all time, Isaac Asimov.

"The tough-guy detective, where the hero is constantly drinking without destroying his liver, constantly having his skull cracked with a pistol without destroying his brain, and constantly shooting down all the characters but one and then pinning the crime on the survivor."

With all due respect and admiration to you, Mr Asimov; Through your work you taught a young boy about the stars, robots and empires in space. Thank you.

Lance Horsman

TV FUTURE

TV FUTURE

The television was on.

People were walking slowly past a camera, their faces sombre. Many had tears rolling down their faces. For others, grief was an expressionless mask. Some carried banners or held posters. Their star had died.

The camera blurred, as if streaked with its own tears, and as its blur faded, music came on, soft and slow. A person emerged from the slowly trudging throng: Lynda Taratello, the anchorperson for *Starwatch at Eight*. She mourned in a tight, black leather skirt and a jacket to match, her cheeks aglow with a healthy wash of tears, mascara slightly smudged.

The music stopped, and – holding her microphone limply in her hand, like an injured ferret – she began to eulogise the loss of a star:

"Today your favourite film crew comes to you live from Marachino Square, where the procession held in honour of the late and undoubtedly great life show star, Freddy Mays, has begun.

"This is Lynda Taratello for *Starwatch at Eight*. As you can see behind me, thousands of people have gathered here today to pay tribute to this compassionate man, who used whatever power he had to touch the lives of others, in a manner which they would never forget. Born in–"

The screen exploded. The second gunshot blew off the top, right-hand corner of the screen, and the large-panel TV fell from its stand and onto the floor of the window display.

In the street, the maniac howling laughter of two drunken gang members in leather and studs rang through the night, shortly joined by more gunshots into the air, and the revving of their bike engines. The leader on the front bike, a big man covered in piercings and gleaming neon dragon tattoos, holstered his gun and raised a bottle in salute.

"Here's to switching off the fucking TV!" He took a big slug of his drink before he threw the bottle into what was left of the showroom window.

*

CHAPTER 1:
THE GRIND

The club was a thick haze of drifting smoke. Neon wall signs buzzed on and off again in the most lazy fashion, and sometimes they flickered irrationally. It added to the feeling of chaos and general lack of care this close to the Rejuvenation.

Down here, this close to the cataclysmic social failure that was the Emera City Rejuvenation Project, repairs and maintenance were low on everybody's agenda. It was always dark, because the lights kept breaking and the power kept cutting. It was always messy, because the trash wasn't collected, the drug addicts spilled into the streets out of darkened alleyways, and gangs set cars and buildings on fire in the middle of running street battles. The Rejuvenation was an apocalyptic fallen hive of concrete slums, a salute to corruption and failed governance in every possible form.

You know how some people feel that the grass is always greener on the other side? Well, from down here, the grass *was* always greener on the other side, because there was no grass left on this side anymore. This side of the proverbial fence, the grass was asphalt and the cows were damaged vending machines. The actual fence was two storeys high, with barbed wire and minigun placements, and the farmer was a pimp in a purple, velvet jumpsuit with heavy, bitch-slap rings and an afro.

James P Holloway, a man who gently fraternised with optimism, believed that the grass was greener on the other side – firstly because it simply couldn't get any worse than it was on this side, but also because, once upon a time, he had believed in it. It occurred to him that life could get better, but then it also occurred to him that he was often wrong about a whole lot of things – like general life choices, for example. This was why his Saturday night was spent walking through a nightclub two streets away from the Rejuvenation, looking for criminals.

The club was full tonight. A rusty steel bar counter ran down the one side of the room. Directly opposite, also running the length of the long, narrow room, was a shelf – a thin wooden plank on a heavy steel I-beam bolted into the wall. A line of tatty and mismatched bar stools collected around the shelf like groupies outside a band's changing room. The stools were all full.

Jim wondered if, since the world was stuck in the quagmire of modern living, with grey slums, cheap noodles, and even cheaper entertainment streaming in through a panel on the wall... was it even worth chasing after a dream if all it contained was plastic cows, asphalt grass, and bitch-slap pimps? There had to be more, but somedays, Jim wasn't so sure anymore.

Down from the bar, the music blared loud and hard. The dancefloor was a miasma of chaos where people could forget themselves. Bass beats thumping so hard that thought was impossible. Bodies pressed so tight against the next sweating body that anonymity was guaranteed. Steaming sweat mingling with the cough of the fog machine, the dancefloor was a drug-induced pall touched by a Puck unleashed from Oberon's command. Jim stayed away from the dancefloor – there was no way he was going to get sucked into that. No doubt it was laced with uppers, downers, and everything else in between, perspired out into a steaming human mist.

Everyone and their dog was here tonight. It was loud and chemical and everybody was on something. Jim had a sip of his ice-cool whiskey, and clinked the glass back down accurately onto its coaster. He looked at his watch. It was about time. They hadn't come out yet. Jim began to feel uneasy. Just a little. Like first-date kind of uneasy.

He smiled a wryly, and shook his head. If they didn't come out, he would have to go in. That made things a lot more difficult.

"Another drink, sir?" The barman reached for the empty glass.

"Ah, no." Jim looked quickly towards the doors facing the dancefloor, then back at the barman, and his empty glass. "No, thanks. One's fine."

The barman moved on.

Jim sat for a while, staring into vacant space, thinking.

There was still the question of cows and grass. He liked the idea that somewhere there was a perfect black and white cow who chewed perfectly green grass in a meadow where life was still and the sun shone across blue skies onto a farmhouse that was safe. Around this house was a garden so free that children would talk about it until they grew old, and would seek to build the same garden for their children. Or maybe it was just a fantasy that lived inside his head. Something he repeated to himself so he could get through the kind of things he did. Or was just about to do.

With one eye firmly appraising the musty patch of darkness opposite the dancefloor, Jim stood up. A single, black door stood in that patch of shadow, its exterior covered in Naugahyde and black plastic buttons. Its handle was a solid brass ball above a keyhole, and there was a slot right in the middle of the door, three-quarters of the way up. The slot was a half a foot wide. Give or take an inch or two.

Beneath his crumpled coat, Jim Holloway felt the weight of his guns sitting against his chest. He had a big one for his right hand and an equally big one for his left hand. They each held 12 shiny bullets capable of piercing anything but the most illegal and hard-to-get hides, and mangling whatever was on the insides into bolognese. Jim stood up grimly and wiped a lone bead of sweat from his forehead. He sauntered over to the door.

Five people had gone into the room behind that door. Half an hour later, another two had gone in. That totalled seven. Three were known addicts, two were drug peddlers, and one was his informant. The only real problem he had was with the seventh. He had never seen her before. Nice looking, in a dark-haired, Latino sort of way – but nothing about her stood out apart from a pretty face. He had nothing on her. There was something about her that he couldn't quite place. It just sort of put him on edge, something which he couldn't figure out. Of course, the whole deal made him nervous anyway. It was a nervous sort of business.

According to his informant, they should have been out in 15 minutes or less – the offenders with the drugs, the peddlers with the marked bills, and the informant with a confession and a plea bargain to get him back on the streets again. It had all sounded very neat and tidy. Wham, bam, thank you ma'am; all nice and rosy. Jim reached the door, and pulled out his guns, two big shiny chunks sitting menacingly in his hands. A young woman with a strange hairdo of pink and blue spikes and a matching bodysuit so tight it could have been spraypainted on, scattered out of his way. Nice bod right there, he thought to himself – it was people like her that made being single just a little harder.

And then he kicked the door in.

"Okay, you pieces of shit…"

A gunshot rang out. The lights went out. Jim dived for the floor, the gunge-covered carpet grazing his elbow through his coat as he fell. His guns were already blazing, firing indiscriminately into the darkness.

Some screams, some shouting, and some more shots followed. Most of them from Jim. He heard someone else scream good and proper scream, and smelt the rich scent of blood pumping thick into the air. Got one.

"My gut! He got me in the gut! Aaah, fuck! I'm gonna die…"

"Shut up, Kramer! For God's sake, shut the fuck up – he'll kill us all if you don't shut up!"

Jim took a guess as to where the voice was coming from, and he squeezed off a couple more shots, rolling off as the return fire came volleying in. He'd heard a fleshy, chunking sound – scratch one more.

The door swung slowly shut behind him. Now the darkness was complete. It was pitcher than pitch and every shadow held menace. Those few short seconds of black air and silence held enough tension for a lifetime of hard knocks.

"Damnit," Jim swore to himself quietly. He knew he was about to crack. He thought that maybe he'd try being nice, just once.

"Okay, you fuckers, this is Jim P Holloway. Yeah, you heard me. THAT Jim Holloway. You know who I am, and you know that you don't have a chance. So if you give up now, we'll all walk out smiling. But if–"

"Shut up…"

"Shoot him! Aaah, shoot him! It's Holloway – we're all gonna die!"

"Shut up, already, I told ya!"

A couple more gunshots rang out, but Jim had rolled away. He wasn't as dumb as he looked.

Okay, so much for Mr Nice Guy. He pulled his cigarette box out of his pocket and crumpled it into a ball. They heard him moving and some more shots rang out, but they missed. One shot came awfully close, though. They seemed to be grouped towards one corner, but there was no way that he could tell for sure – not without some sort of light.

He lit his cigarette box and threw it towards the corner. As he lit, he rolled, picked up his gun and shot. The other gun came up and shot. Roll, move, shoot; roll, move, shoot. Just like he had been trained. Bullets chunked into the floor all around him, but these guys were amateurs. Jim wasn't.

There were four of them clustered in the corner. Roll, shoot, shoot.

Three. Roll, move, dive, shoot.

Two. Move, move, shoot.

One. Blam, blam, blam.

And then there were none.

Click click click.

He was out of ammo – and just in time. By his count, that made six. Only one more.

There was a rustle from the other corner. He turned towards it, and a figure loomed up dark and rushing towards him. It bowled into him, a knife slashing at his hand as he tried to grab on. Jim fell back, and dived at it again. This time, though, the knife caught him in the stomach as he and the figure tumbled to the ground in a flurry of coats and blood and hair and limbs. As they hit the ground, the woman got up and ran off again, the door opening and coloured light, smoke, and sound from the club spilling into the room. Jim dived for the doorway and pulled himself through, losing sight of her in the fog of the club. Or maybe it was the fog in his head. No, he was in pain. Jim clutched at his stomach with more than a little surprise.

The bitch, she'd caught him a good one.

Weakly, Jim reached into his pocket for his phone. Blood was pumping through his fingers and no matter how hard he tried to hold it back, more just seemed to come out of the big gash in his belly. He got up onto his knees now and the carpet beneath him darkened with his blood.. A spreading ink of darkness. His fingers stumbled for numbers as they slipped across the face of his phone. Shit, wrong number. He dialled again.

"Bounty Depot, hello?"

"It's Jim Holloway. I'm at The Grind."

"The nightclub?"

"Yeah."

"Oh my God, Jim. What's…"

The last thing Jim remembered before dropping the phone and falling into his own blood, was that his jaw hurt from clenching his teeth.

"…wrong? Hello? Jim?"

*

CHAPTER 2: HOW THINGS BEGIN

The cows were all plastic and the grass was all Astroturf. They were Friesland cows. Jim was there, and he had a gun in his hand. His gun. He was trying to shoot the cows, but somehow, the gun wouldn't work. It kept on clicking. The cows began to beep. A loud, pinging sort of sound, in a slow, steady rhythm. Damn those pinging cows.

Jim woke up.

The machine next to his bed continued to ping and beep. It tubed into his side, and pumped something vile and yellow out of the other end. Aah, the organ support system. Modern technology was truly amazing, Jim mused to himself.

"Jim."

He looked up to see Irma, the secretary from the depot. And Wilcox, his superior. Or rather, his contracted boss. Jim nodded his head as best he could.

"Hey, Jim," Wilcox beamed from behind Irma. "Well done on those six."

"Yes, well done," echoed Irma, leaning over to put some flowers on the table, her 36-Ds pushing almost right up against Jim's face. He started to get a hard-on.

"Listen up, big shooter," said Wilcox. "I can only pay you half for each of those offenders you bagged, because they're dead. They were MFI – Marked for Incarceration, not for Termination. One form is blue; the other one is green. Look, you know the deal – company policy and all that. Also, one of them was a registered informant, so technically you should pay *us* for the loss of his services, but I'm willing to let that slide, seeing how you got gutted like a fish and you need the money to pay for your new stomach."

Wilcox was a company man through and through. That meant he went by the book as long as it suited him. Sometimes it even suited the company. He never let anything "slide", unless it was the lube for the monstrous corporate shaft you were about to catch. Jim's hard-on started to subside.

"Anyways," Wilcox went on. "The six dead ones aren't the problem; it's the one live one that got away. She's the hassle. In fact, she's a big hassle."

Jim raised his eyebrow curiously.

Wilcox faltered. "Er, actually, I'm not too sure of all the details. But what I do know is that after you went down, the green and whites arrived, opened their usual public disturbance report, and fed this chick's description into the system. So far, everything's run of the mill. But a short while later, some grey suits come down from Agora-1 and take over the handling of the case. Turns out this chick who carved your stomach is some sort of classified happening, and you're the only government employee who's ever met her and lived long enough to light a cigarette afterwards." Wilcox motioned to Irma. "Get me that water jug there please, honey."

Jim pushed himself up into an almost sitting position. He shook his head. "Fred," he croaked through a dry and tired throat. "You know I'm not a government employee." Sometimes Wilcox needed reminding of how things *actually* were, rather than how he thought they were. Otherwise, the situation could well get out of hand, which Jim had the suspicious feeling was about to happen anyway.

"Well, yes, Jim, you're quite right there, of course. You're freelance – I get it. But you are contracted to us for another 48 hours, and that makes you ours – technically speaking, of course – for two more days. Besides, who's to say that you won't renew your contract for one more week? You've run for 13 consecutive weeks before, plenty times. Hell, haven't you done as many as 20? I mean, don't you hold some sort of record?"

"Yeah," Irma smiled at Jim, handing Wilcox a glass of water. "Twenty-one weeks. Most ever in the department's history, Fred."

"That's right!" Wilcox took the water from Irma. "The most ever in Emera, but not as much as John Centauri of Alpha system. He did 33 weeks until some crazy blew his leg off." Wilcox paused. "Say, Jim, don't you and Johnny Centauri have some sort of history together? Childhood pals or something?"

Jim's lips tightened sharply.

"Anyway," Wilcox ploughed on. "Now he's got a vat-grown leg. You know how they are with replacements these days, Jim." He paused for a sip. "Aaah, that is good. But hell, of course you know what I mean. Am I speaking to Mr Cyber-stomach or what?"

"Is that it?" Jim croaked.

"Actually, no, Jim." Wilcox downed the rest of the glass's contents. "Now, I know you're the best – and the grey guys upstairs know it too. That's why one of them wants to have a little word with you sometime soon. Perhaps make you an offer you can't refuse, or something? So I just dropped by to give you a bit of advanced notice and to ask you to maybe behave decently for once and not like some *yippee-ki-yay* asshole who doesn't give a shit about anything."

Jim groaned inwardly. Not the grey men. Shit, he was tired. He wanted some time by himself to piece things together. He looked up at Fred Wilcox and nodded.

"Okay. Now you can go. I'm tired."

"Righto, fine. I'll tell them to drop by sometime soon," said Wilcox, turning for the door. "Cheers, Jim."

"Yeah, cheers, Jim," said Irma, planting a kiss on his cheek and then sauntering out after Wilcox.

Jim relaxed back into his pillow and fell asleep, dreaming of grey men chasing Irma's behind in an Astroturf field full of cows with vat-grown legs.

*

"Hi, Lynda. Nice show tonight."

Lynda turned to thank whoever was behind her, but by the time she did, they were lost in the throng rapidly disappearing beneath her.

Level 42. This was the first time she'd ever been asked up to level 42. She got off the escalator and turned to board the one which would take her up the next two levels of the massive, spiraling column that supported the inside of the sparkling Horscht and Beckenworth building. She was approaching level 20, and as she got higher, the crowds were visibly thinning. Tough at the top, crowded at the bottom – that's what her producer used to say. That was before he dived off the edge of his 38th-level apartment balcony and apricot-jammed his head all over the pavement almost a quarter mile below.

Lynda caught a glimpse of herself in one of the many

glossy mirrored walls, and quickly pulled her hand away from her head. She had been twirling again. Whenever she was nervous, she twirled her hair between her fingers. She gently pushed the offending lock back into its place and inspected herself in the next approaching mirrored wall. Hmm, not bad. Her hair was suitably blonde; her dress suitably tight. Her personal imager had told her that 63.2% of television viewers preferred blonde hair this year, and so she had blonde hair, in the style that 44.75% of people thought the most appealing. Her ratings had upped 15 points in the last two months.

Added to that, her new scriptwriter was a whiz kid, and one of her shows had even been dubbed "insightful" by Storm Wesseberg, possibly one of the most hardnosed critics on the Western Seaboard. She was going up, alright – in more ways than one.

After level 25, the wide-berthed escalators stopped their vine-like creep around the building's central column and gave way to a set of glass-tubed elevators. Sleek, silver-tinted oblong tubes that to her had always looked like big metal capsules sliding up and down a slender glass throat. The man at the door greeted her as she stopped, and asked for her guest card. She pulled it out of her small, red Gucci bag and gave it to him. He nodded and fed it into the slot.

His uniform was slightly worn at the elbows, and his jaunted cap showed beneath it a creeping patch of baldness. He turned around and gave her back the card, his eyes meeting hers for just a brief glimpse before they averted to his control console again. His eyes were deep and brown, framed with wrinkles. She wondered what those eyes had seen in their time. No doubt he had many tales to tell. There was a possible story in that; Lynda made a mental note to tell her story team about this guy.

The rushing of the elevator slowed and the doors silently glided open, revealing the passageway to one of five apartments this high up. Lynda marvelled to herself – her entire apartment could fit in the elevator lobby. She walked out, and a new wave of excitement swept over her. Okay, Lynda, she thought to herself. You're cool. It's nothing big. You can handle this. But it is the big time.

If things went well for her tonight, she could be on the road to something big – bigger than she could possibly ever have imagined.

*

Two weeks of hospital food is never a pleasant thing. The new stomach lining didn't help, either. Ah well, Jim mused. With the number of ulcers he had, he'd have had to get a new stomach sometime soon anyway. He looked down at the yellow-papered official forms in front of him, trying to translate the legalese in the fine print.

"James P Holloway?" Someone called him. The voice was flat with a slight nasal twang, and it was issued from somewhere behind him.

Jim turned around. "Yup?"

It was a short, grey man in an ill-fitting grey suit and cheap sunglasses. It seemed to Jim that special agents had a monopoly on bad taste. And they all looked the same, as if they were pumped out of some great big machine that mass-produced cheap lead figurines.

"Flint's the name." The agent held up an ID card in one hand, and held out the other for Jim to shake. Jim took the smaller man's hand in his meaty grip. It was surprisingly firm.

"I presume, Mr Holloway, that your superior, Officer

Wilcox, informed you of the situation at present?"

"He's not my superior," said Jim. "My contract ended ten days ago, and I didn't renew."

A flicker of annoyance tattled its way across the agent's face.

"Okay, fine. He's not your superior. But I presume that he did tell you about the woman?"

"Well, yes, he did. But he didn't say much..."

The agent cut in: "That's because he didn't know much, Mr Holloway."

Jim stopped and turned back to the hospital release forms in front of him. Once he'd finished signing them, he looked back up at the agent. "So, let me guess, Mr Government Agent..."

The grey man nodded his head.

"...You're going to fill me in on the small works about this chick and give me some sort of once-in-a-lifetime, I-can-never-refuse offer to track her down, because I am the best there is and too many government agents have already bit the bullet because of her. How about that?"

"Not too bad," said Flint. "You're not as dumb as you look."

"Up yours," said Jim gracefully.

"So anyway," the agent ignored Jim's last comment. "You interested, or what?" He reached into his blazer pocket and pulled out a thick, folded, green sheath of paper. "This here is her P433 form."

Jim knew the form well. It was the staple food of his paperwork diet. The P433 – <u>M</u>arked for <u>U</u>ntimely <u>T</u>ermination form. MUT. Mutie. From the government office affectionately known as the Bounty Depot. He perused the form briefly, his eyes lingering on the upper-right corner: TERMINATION PAYMENT: 30 000 ED.

Jim was incredibly interested. For the last six (even though he had gotten only half per MFI), he had made ED1500. One-and-a-half-thousand Emera dollars. He would've made three if everything had gone as it should've, but that damn bitch had stuck him and fouled up everything.

"Okay," he said nonchalantly. "It looks interesting."

"I thought you might say that." The agent looked pleased that he had gotten his own way. He looked like the sort who usually got his own way. "If you stay interested, go see Wilcox. He has the run-down at his office. He'll give us a call when you decide." The grey man turned and left, pausing briefly while the automatic doors slid open to let him out.

*

CHAPTER 3: WE'RE GOING PLACES

Right now, the grass was looking a helluva lot greener and the cows were looking like walking fillet. In fact, to someone peering over the fence, things looked like they almost might be going well in the life of Jim Holloway.

The shuttle took off in a thick, white arc, leaving behind it a jagged, staccato trail of orange, red, and yellow contrasting against the dark-blue sky pin-cushioned with stars and fading into a sleepy black. The hum of the flight station was left behind to a soft rushing feeling, almost like standing underneath a dry waterfall. The station itself – a startling ball of silver – began slowly diminishing, becoming a faraway star and then a blip and then nothing as the shuttle reached its ludicrous speed. It was so fast that it was ludicrous to even think about it.

Jim sank back into his seat. The file on his lap was open, and he had a whiskey and soda in his hand. So, first of all, she wasn't from any of the local systems – maybe that could explain why she had seemed so out of place. She was 26, and she went by the name of Isabella Carla. She had a first name for a surname, and she was also extremely attractive. Jim had never chased better looking prey, in fact. All he had to do was find out where she was, and then bring her in – or put her down. For a record fee.

As for why the government wanted her, he didn't know. Of course, there was some official cock and bull story about her being wanted for trading in sensitive knowledge, apart from her lesser rap sheet, which read like a small booklet on how to be a sociopath. But Jim had been around long enough to know when he was being fed a line, and this one was no different from any of the others he'd ever been fed. Maybe the packaging was a little different, and it was given by the other side of the law – but, at the end of the day, it amounted to the same thing. There was more to this than met the eye, Jim mused.

He picked the file up again.

The fat woman sitting next to him nudged him with her flabby, rounded elbow. "Look there – they're letting down the screen!" She quivered excitedly beneath her blue and white floral, dress-shaped tent. "They're putting on the life shows!" She wriggled impatiently in her seat, a gesture more suited to little girls than people who weighed just less than a small car. She bumped him again, and this time some of his whiskey jumped out of the glass and onto his crotch.

Jim laughed and shook his head. He knew that it had just been waiting for a moment like that. Trust his luck.

The fat woman didn't even notice that she'd caused him to spill on himself; she was glued to the screen that was gradually slipping – degree by tantalising degree – out of the ceiling of the shuttle. Almost unconsciously, the woman's hand snaked down to her handbag and fished out a chocolate bar that she raised to the glistening pink vacuum of her mouth in a well-practiced motion.

Jim knew he was a bit overweight, but this woman was disgusting.

The hostess, a tall woman in a blue suit, armed with a

smile painted on with too much red lipstick, came by and told them that for the next four hours, they would present the daily life shows. Then, after a brief break, they would screen another four-hour batch made up of *Starwatch at Eight, Stargaze, Star-gatherer*, and an excerpt from *Voyeur: The Inside Views from the Stars who Make News*.

Jim, ever the gentleman, thanked the hostess, got out of his seat, and went over to the bar, sitting with his back to the TV.

*

At first glance, Jim didn't like the look of Alpha-1. It was too neat. The spaceport shone like a new car, and its plastic seats even had that new car smell, which was great if it was your new car. The staff had smiley nametags, and all responded when you called them by their first names. The drinks at the spaceport bar were expensive. The climatic control kept the temperature at just too hot to wear a long coat, but not hot enough to warrant taking it off.

There were no bums or hawkers, and when he got outside of the spaceport, a taxi pulled up smoothly and without having to cut off a number of its competitors. Worst of all, it was a droid-driven cab. Disgustedly, Jim threw his bag on the back seat, and got in.

"Good day, sir," a female voice soothed gently over the speaker behind his head. "My name is Melody, and I'll be your driver for the day. If you have a destination in mind, name it and I can give you the approximate cost in any of the registered ESU currencies. If you have no definite destination, then I also have a comprehensive city-wide grid map, which is currently being displayed in front of you."

A screen flickered to life in front of Jim with an innocuous ping.

"Thank you for your custom, and please respect the sanctity of this cab, as it is my home. Peace be with you."

"Yeah, whatever." Jim stared at the grid map for a short while.

"Okay, Doris, take me to City Hall, level..." he paused to finger a reading on the map. "...thirteen. And I want to use your phone and also your directory."

"Yes, sir," said the cab.

Jim felt the cab's engines vibrate to life as it slowly lurched forwards and upwards.

"And by the way, sir," the cab continued. "My name is Melody. You mustn't forget that android mechanisms have feelings, too."

The cab surged ahead smoothly and efficiently, buildings whizzing by above and beneath it, as they approached the centre of Alpha-1: the city hall. The city hall of Alpha-1 was a megalithic structure, even by the standards of the day. At 220 storeys, it stood tall and proud above the rest of the city, a symbol of the strong hope and might with which the city had been founded. It had glistening, white sides and a rounded dome top. Jim thought it looked like a 200-storey dildo. It was, however, the hub in a bureaucratic hive responsible for the lives of over 30 million people.

Split into 20 sections, each consisting of ten floors (with the other 20 storeys being comprised of support shafts and stabilisers and atmospheric maintainers), the city hall was in fact, a city within a mega-city. The 13th level – slightly over halfway up – was one of the quietest levels, with most of the smaller, inconsequential departments silently going about their daily grind, wedged between the convenient-to-the-public lower levels and the high-prestige upper levels. Jim's destination was on the 133rd floor, the Alpha City Serious Crime Deterrent Department. The politically correct term for the Bounty Depot.

Bing.

"We have reached your destination, sir," said Melody in her politest and least offensive voice. "Please remain seated until the docking procedure is 100% complete. That will be 25.50. Thank you for travelling with me, and peace be with you."

Jim fed two twenties into the slot as Melody rocked to a gentle halt, her vertical vents shuddering off fine jets of white steam against the slick, black docking platform. The door opened with a small pneumatic jerk, and the steam dissipated into warm droplets of moist grease on the platform, making it even slicker.

Jim got out and proceeded to his meeting place.

*

He didn't know what to expect from Johnny Centauri. It had been a long time, and time could do strange things to a man.

It had changed Johnny. From friend to enemy; from family to foe. Over the years, Jim had heard so much about the guy, he was almost a living legend. Mind you, the same thing could be said about Jim.

He was, after all, THE Jim Holloway. He didn't die. Beat him, stab him, shoot him – Jim Holloway was tougher than Rasputin. And meaner, too. Because if you didn't finish the job, then he would come back and get you. No one had ever finished the job, and so he always came back. No matter who, no matter how. No doubt, of course, similar things were muttered about Johnny in the seedier dives of

Alpha-1, and that was why Jim needed this man. The man he'd once called friend.

Jim made his way to the restaurant on the far side of the Alpha-1 building, floor 133. It was a little Italian place – a red, white, and green awning hanging over the front door, and a violin concerto playing softly over the casual supper talk of the customers. There were strings of garlic hanging down the doorposts, and the sharp smell of tomato steamed from the kitchen and pinched at his nose. He suddenly realised he was hungry.

The waiter – a short, wide man with no hair, a moustache, and some light red stains on his white shirt – led Jim to a shadow-strewn booth in the corner. Johnny was already there.

"John," Jim nodded in greeting.

"Jimmy," Johnny did likewise, as Jim tucked into his seat.

There was a brief moment of silence as the men contemplated each other across the gap of the plastic table between them. The candle on the table flickered in the red light and the half-shadows cast by the booth partitions and the Italian-styled lighting. The booth next to them was bathed in green. Jim lit a cigarette and put the pack back into his pocket.

"You going to offer me one of those?" Johnny broke the silence, his whispered voice barely making it across the gap between them. He'd once had his throat cut.

Jim retrieved the box and matches and slid them across the table. "You're not a smoker, John. When did you start?"

John removed a cigarette and lit it. "Too long ago, Jim." He slid the pack and matches back across the table. Jim left them where they were.

There was another moment's pause, this time broken by Holloway. "So, how've you been?"

Johnny waved his hand. "Ah, you know. So-so. I'm still alive," he concluded, almost as if reassuring himself. "The other day some punk took my leg off. It was the closest I've ever been to..." he faltered. "To almost not making it..."

"Yeah, I heard."

"It was raining and five of them took me by surprise." John shrugged to himself. "The rain was so damn thick and the shadows were so damn dark I couldn't see anything, Jim. Maybe before I woulda been more careful or something, but I dunno. I guess I've just been winning for so long, I forgot to be careful, you know? Or maybe I wanted to die. The shrink – they gave me a head doctor after the hospital, can you believe that? – he reckons that I wanted to die; that after ten years doing what we do, he reckons we all want to die. Death is a way of life for us. We choose it to punish ourselves for our evil, he says. What shit – can you believe that? Me, I want to die? Nah, you know me, Jim..." John paused. "Well, you knew me once." He thought for a while. "I don't want to die, do I?" He didn't sound sure.

"Nah. What the fuck does a shrink know about anything, anyway?" Jim said, but his heart wasn't in it, because there were many days when he too woke up doubting himself. On those days, he had to give himself a reason to live. One day, the only reason he didn't pull out his guns and turn them on himself was simply because he didn't want to die looking like some lonely, fat guy. He had to lose weight first. Another day, he was interrupted by the postman. Maybe the shrink had a point.

"Well, you know, John," Jim went on. "Things with me, they've been pretty bad too. Some bitch damn near left me dead on a lousy dancefloor with my guts around my shoes. And you know what?"

Johnny waited for him to carry on.

"I didn't give a shit that I was dying. The only reason I wanted to live was so that I could come back and nail her blue slip to the wall."

"Did you?"

"Not yet, but I will. But you know what I think it is, John? The reason why guys like you and me don't give a damn?"

This time, John answered. "What?"

"Because what the hell do we have to give a damn about? Think about it. Remember when we first started, you and me together – we used to give a damn. Then along came Marge, and things bombed out a bit. I won't get into that. You were there; you know how it went. I left for Emera, and you and she come out here to make a clean start of it. Get away from the memories.

"For the first few years, the only thing that kept me going was the hate. Shit, I hated you, man. Hell, I hated Marge too – and loved her at the same time. If it wasn't hate that kept me going, then it was the confusion. Sometimes I didn't even know what day of the week it was, or even if it was night or day. To tell the truth, I didn't care. Now they were bad reasons to keep going, I admit, but they were reasons. And then, after a few more years, it was just a rut I was stuck in. I'd pull out of it; I always did – well, that's what I told myself, anyway. But I didn't. And then I just stopped caring. Not straight away. Not all at once. Just one day I woke up and realised that at some point I'd stopped giving a shit about anything, and I didn't know when or why."

Johnny Centauri nodded his head of closely cropped hair, his face in a sour grimace. "Yeah, that sounds about right. Except my hate came a couple years later, after Marge died. But I never hated you, Jim. Not the same way you hated me."

"That's only because you never had a reason to, like I

did."

"Fair enough," conceded Johnny. He had a fair point.

"So tell me then, Jim," John looked pointedly at him. "Seeing as how we're sitting here like we're genteel corporate workers that don't get paid to kill other people for a living, and we're swapping yarns, tell me: do you still hate me?"

Jim hesitated. He'd played this scenario over in his head more than a few times, and it sometimes ended up with Johnny dead, sometimes with himself dead, and sometimes with both of them dead. He smiled and shook his head. "Nah, Johnny. I don't hate you anymore. Ten years is a long time to hate someone – even a cold shit like you."

Johnny's face split into that short, tight-lipped grin of his. "It's good to hear that, Jim, coz I don't think I would've enjoyed killing you."

"Likewise," said Jim.

There was a pause.

"Say," said Jim, picking up the menu. "What's the food like in this dump?"

"Pretty good," said John.

"Right. Well, let's order something to eat, because I'm starving. Then I'll tell you the real reason why I'm here."

"Okay," said John. "That sounds fine to me."

*

CHAPTER 4: KEEP YOUR ENEMIES CLOSE

The suns were setting. Three of them, out of a mostly azure sky which faded from black on the one end, to purple-red with flashes of white wedged in between the three aging orbs on the other. It was breathtakingly beautiful. Slowly, like golden treacle down the side of a jar, they sank behind a small, green hill at the foot of which sat Jim's house. It was a quaint, happy little house, with a white picket fence. Two dogs and a cow. The cow was on the other side of the fence, where the grass seemed distinctly greener. Somehow, though, Jim didn't seem to mind.

And he knew why, for there was a woman in his dream. He couldn't see her or hear her, but somehow, in that uncanny way that you know these things when you dream, he knew that she was there.

At first, there was nothing but the sound of a gentle wind rustling across the turf. Then, something: he heard her footsteps on the grass. Her breathing; her white dress blowing in that same wind. He hadn't seen her, but he knew that her dress was white. It had to be. And as she neared, he smelt her – she smelt of coconut and sun oil. Of warm, tanned skin, and a light, airy smell which reminded him of fruit. It was the sort of smell that made him feel all good inside. She reached him and lovingly wrapped her arms around his waist, her chin draped over his shoulder. Jim felt her body press softly up against his from behind…

He woke up.

It was morning in John's apartment, and the wan light through the windows painted the place a creamy white, making it look like an old, corroded photograph. John's atmospheric control unit was down, and instead of programming the windows for sunrise glow, they had been programmed for pale mid-afternoon sun on a cloudy day. It was always cloudy in John's apartment.

"Jimmy? You up?" John asked from the kitchen.

"Yup." Jim stared ahead at the wall, still half asleep.

"Coffee?"

"Yup."

"What do you have – sugar, cream, what?"

"Yup. Whatever. Just… caffeine."

"Okay."

Johnny brought two steaming mugs from the kitchen through to the lounge and put one on the table next to Jim.

"Mmmh," Jim grunted by way of thanks, picking up the coffee and downing a scalding sip.

"Shit, that's hot!"

"Well," Johnny mused. "Coffee. It is made with boiling water."

"Okay, you win. I'm up," said Jim. He looked around, as if realising where he was for the first time.

"Say, John, big place you've got here."

John sipped. "Yeah, well… after Marge died, I was going to get rid of the place, you know? Memories and all that. But then I just stopped giving a shit where I stayed. I mean, I was comfy here, and after a while… Marge was dead anyway, you know…"

"Yeah, I know," said Jim. He got up and started rummaging through his bag which he had left against the wall. He pulled out a pack of cigarettes and a shirt which was marginally cleaner than the one in which he'd slept. He slipped it on.

"So Johnny, you know this town. Where do you reckon our girl could be hiding?"

"Not too sure," Johnny shrugged. "But I figure we can kick over a couple rocks and see what crawls out. If she was last seen three days ago, there's only a few places she could've come in – legal or otherwise – so first we can check those out."

"Right. What about safehouses? Where would she hide?"

"Nah, this city's too big to ever find her through that sort of thing. But I know a few people who've got their ear to the ground and maybe they've heard something. You got that picture handy?"

Jim leant over and pulled it out of his coat pocket, stopping as he did so. His eyes passed over the image of her, and a shiver ran down his spine. His vision glued onto the picture and for a split-second, the world around Jim Holloway stopped.

"Say, Jimmy, you okay?"

No answer.

"Jim!" Johnny raised his voice slightly.

Jim shook his head slightly as if clearing some sort of mental fog. Slowly, almost reluctantly, he handed the picture over to his partner.

"What's with you?" John chided.

"I dunno. Somebody just walked across my grave."

"What?"

"Nothing. It was just something a guy I once knew said

whenever he felt the heebie-jeebies."

"Felt the what?"

"Look," Jim said pointedly. "I just felt weird for a second, okay? I don't know what the fuck it was, and I said something that another depot-man used to say whenever he felt shit wasn't going down the way it was meant to. But it didn't help him, coz he died anyway. Okay? There – that's all of it."

"Jesus," said Johnny. "You got up all bright and cheery this morning. I don't know why the fuck I asked. Now, finish your coffee." He got up and walked away, into his bedroom.

*

Agent Spack was having a bad day. It was so bad, in fact, that he knew he was going to die today. He knew with the same sort of certainty that he knew the two suns would rise to the north this morning and set to the south-east later this afternoon. He knew he was going to die, because he was going to kill himself.

"Good morning, Agent Spack," Jeanette, the French nurse, greeted him with a happy smile and a nod of her head. The nod sent a warm ripple down her curly mass of brown hair. "And how are we this morning?"

"'We'," said Agent Spack pointedly, "are fine this morning, Jeanette. 'We' were just wondering how the rest of the world was faring."

"Well, we've got a beautiful day programmed, lots of sun and blue skies…"

"Just like every day, Jeanette. Rising on the one side and setting on the other, two glorious suns, blah, blah, blah, blah…"

"Yes, Agent Spack. Two suns, just like every day – but that's no reason to be so negative about it. It still is a beautiful day, after all." She walked over and started folding the blanket at the bottom of his bed. "Besides, you should consider yourself lucky to be in a place like this. It really is quite lovely."

"Yup," Agent Spack smiled his biggest, beamiest smile. "I must be lucky. That's why I'm stuck in a hospital for fruitcakes and I can't even wipe my own backside without asking for permission."

She moved to the head of the bed and plumped his pillows. "Ah, you're just a pussy cat, Agent Spack; don't you try and act tough. You don't impress me. Anyway, you'll be up and about in no time. The doctors here are very good."

She leant over and kissed him on the forehead, her well-cleaved bust hanging tantalisingly in front of him.

"There we are. Now, isn't that better?" She pouted her cute French pout.

"Yes," Spack had to agree. "That is."

"You be good now, and I'll see you later, Agent Spack. The doctors are coming at 10:30."

She turned and walked out of the room, stopping as she passed through the door. "Oh, and by the way, your paper is on the seat next to you. *Au revoir, mon petit champignon.*"

Spack waved goodbye feebly. "Yes, and bye-bye to you, too."

The door swung slowly shut behind her, and Spack couldn't help but feel that she was right, somehow. He was a little mushroom. And all the agencies were doing was keeping him in the dark and feeding him shit.

Spack fumbled around for a cigarette, lit it, took a deep breath, and slumped back into his pillow. He shut his eyes...

She was in his arms. They were dancing. The world was

spinning around them in a blur of colour and music. There were other people there, but he was lost in her massive, brown eyes. They were in the middle of the Effenberg village hall, but they could've been on the moon as far as he cared. Any moon, anywhere. He was with the love of his life, and she was with him, and he never wanted it to stop – they swirled and danced, the lights spun...

"Ah, shit!"

Spack shook his hand vigorously. The cigarette had burnt down to the stump, and he had singed himself.

Fuck it all, he thought. Fuck everything. He wondered why he couldn't just die.

He had met her in Newspace, on the third moon of a small rim planet – the only reason he remembered the name of the place was because he had met her there. Epiphany. The place was called Epiphany. She had been placed under observation. He had no idea why; he was just to observe, and report, and act on further instructions.

"His was not to reason why/ His was just to do or die..."; "*Dulce et decorum est/ pro patria more...*"

And all that shit.

Well, he had done what he was told to, and now he would die. He was supposed to make accidental contact as he past her, to place the bug – and never see her again. But it hadn't worked out like that. He remembered the way she had lightly brushed his hand with hers. She had smiled, her hand warm on his, apologising for bumping into him – she was so clumsy sometimes. She smiled again, and that made everything alright. He almost felt guilty. And that was it. That was all that had happened. The assignment was over; nothing too taxing.

Five days later, the dreams had started. At first, they had made him happy, but by the time the second week of dreams came, he was dreading sleep because he knew that the dream would end and he'd have to wake up again. Life couldn't compare to these dreams. They were so real; they weren't like dreams at all. They were like life.

By the end of the third week, he couldn't take it anymore. Life just wasn't worth living: there was no point if he couldn't have her. Without her – without the world in his dreams, the possibility, the totally tangible reality of what could be – he would rather be dead. It was totally unbelievable, but in the space of three weeks he had slipped from an inscrutably efficient agency-trained instrument of death with an outstanding service record and impeccable reputation amongst his peers… to a delusional, insomniac, weepy, suicidal wreck. A fruitcake, basically.

It was sometime around that stage that he'd got up from his desk, walked over to his window, and jumped out. Thirty-five storeyss. You would've thought that would do the job. But five storeys down, he'd hit the roof of a car, knocking himself unconscious and breaking half the ribs on the left side of his body.

Now, strapped into a hospital bed, under the influence of a veritable cocktail of suppressive drugs, life was hell. He wanted to die. In fact, he *needed* to die. He just wanted to know why they gave so much of a shit to keep him alive.

*

They sat in silence as they headed out to Metrospace Inc, one of the three spaceports around the city. John skimmed through a little black book and Jim sat in contemplation of his previous night's dream and the events which had followed. He had never felt anything like it before. The dream was so real it had scared him, and when he had seen

Isabella's picture, something in him had just given way. It was as if he had looked into a mirror expecting to see his own reflection, and somebody else had looked back at him – and he didn't know why. Their cab (Janet was its name) stopped, offered them a good day, and informed them that they owed her 54 Alpha standards. Johnny slid a card into the slot, they got out, and she hovered off into the smoggy morning haze.

Johnny put the little black book into his pocket.

"What's the deal with the book?" Jim motioned at John's pocket.

"My tag book," said John. "You know – who's tagged to who, how many kids they got…"

"Yeah, what's their favourite ball team, who's done them dirty…"

"Right. That sort of thing."

"So then," Jim started as he held open the glass door for Johnny and the woman behind them. "Who have we come to visit?"

"Miles Berman. Works in security. If your lady had to show any sort of plastic, ID, anything – he's the man who would've seen it."

"What's he like, this Berman guy?"

"Nah, he's pretty much harmless," said John. "Likes to think he's some sort of military material, but he's basically a security guard with a bit of clout. Give him a uniform and a nightstick and all of a sudden he thinks he's Mr Universe – you know the sort."

"Yup." Jim nodded. He knew the sort.

They made their way through the main departures hall of Metrospace. It was more the sort of thing Jim was used to: crumpled polystyrene cups around the coffee machine, plastic wrappers on the floor, a half-asleep guy with a paunch using his mop to rearrange the dirt and keep the floors slippery. Jim beamed a big smile at him as they walked past.

*

They sat in one of the plastic-seated takeaways that lined the arrivals hall of Metrospace Inc. Johnny was most of the way through a large serving of chips with sauerkraut and Jim was busy with a mouthful of his second hamburger.

Linda Blakes was a happily married mother of two, away on a business trip, and very eager to get back home to her snot-nosed kids and real estate salesman husband. She was an attractive, dark-haired woman. And she didn't exist.

Jim was impressed. The copy of her ID card in his hand looked just like the real thing. To duplicate or fake an ID card these days was a virtual impossibility. Each card had its own magnetic coding, laser-cut etch encryption, four different types of computerized, tamper-proof software systems onboard, as well as unique watercolour and paper-blend enciphering. The only way to get a card of the quality he held in his hand was for the government to give you one. It was a very good copy.

"So?" John regarded Jim with a slightly bemused expression and half a mouthful of sauerkraut. "I'm stumped, Jim. I don't see how she could've gotten such a high-quality ID like that, unless that's her real one. It's that simple."

"Unless," countered Jim, "she was given one."

"What? Now government agencies are standing on street corners and handing out ID cards for 50 bucks a piece? Nah, Jim. I don't buy it."

"Well, it's a possibility. But okay. Say you're right. Say it's a heap of shit, then. Then what? What can you come up with?"

Johnny wiped a spot of mustard off his chin. "To tell the truth, I don't know what to make of it. I've never seen anything like it. But if there is any sort of government involvement, then I think the only way to check it out is to run that card by a couple friends of mine down at City Hall, and one or two guys on the beat. If she's used a taxicab, a hospital, a police car, or basically just about anything, there's a good chance they've got it on record somewhere. I don't know... maybe we can try and pick up her trail from there?"

Jim nodded. "Maybe. Well, you do that, John. I think I'll pay a visit to the nearest agency depot. I've got one or two questions of my own that I need answered." Jim stood up and wiped his hands on his coat. "You get this one, Johnny. I'll meet you back at your place later."

"Yeah, okay, Jim. But..."

"Cheers, John."

Jim walked out of the takeaway. He had a hunch, and if he had learnt anything over the past ten years of killing criminals who most certainly didn't want to die, it was that you got two types of hunches: one was a lump on your back, and the other was a message from somebody upstairs. And that didn't mean the apartment above yours.

*

The door to Manny Dryer's apartment swung open automatically in front of Lynda like a fairy godmother's wand. She stepped in apprehensively, not quite knowing what to expect.

A tall, spindle-thin man dressed in a butler's suit and

a small smirk glided up to her silently and machine-like along the purple-cushioned walls of Manny Dryer's residence. It seemed that there was no accounting for bad taste.

"Good day, Madame Taratello," said the butler in a slightly clipped accent. "I am Basque, Mr Dryer's manservant. This way, please."

Basque turned on his heel and walked from the door down a tubular, semi-circled passageway. With a small swish, the door shut automatically behind her. Two doors down the way, Basque stopped and motioned for Lynda to enter.

"Through here please, madam." He made a small nodding motion with his head, which looked to Lynda as if he was a tall building beginning to sway. She almost giggled nervously.

"This is Mr Dryer's leopard lounge, madam. Please make yourself comfortable. There are drinks in the cabinet over by the far wall, if you wish. Mr Dryer will be with you shortly." He nodded his head ever so slightly, and walked off.

Lynda looked around. Judging only by the passageway and this room, this had to be the biggest apartment she had ever seen in her life. There were mirrors on the black, star-speckled ceiling, and the lounge suites were some sort of leather in leopard print. On the glass-topped and black-framed coffee table, there sat a tinted purple glass sculpture of a naked woman riding a large stallion. In the golden wall unit against the far wall there sat an array of small, brass ornaments and idols, including an erotic chess set, the pieces carved to look like naked women and phallic symbols. There was a red and orange lava lamp in the corner.

Lynda sank down into the plush, leather lounge suite, and waited for Manny Dryer.

A short few minutes later, he walked in.

Manny was the short, agitated, tanned sort of man who spoke nervously and quickly and was always wiping his hand across his forehead, smoothing the last errant strands of his black hair back into place. He wore a turquoise-blue silk shirt with the sleeves rolled up past skinny forearms that jingled with heavy gold bracelets, and were covered with thick, blue veins usually seen on heroin addicts and the terminally nervous.

He paused, threw three thick manilla envelopes down onto the coffee table, walked over to the bar counter, and pulled a drink out of the fridge.

Manny wrenched the tab, took a long pull at the can, then came over to where Lynda was sitting. He put the can on the table and wiped his hand on his cream-coloured pants. "Well, I'll be a porcupine in a needle factory." He wiped his forehead. "It's been a long day, Lynda. Hi, I'm Manny Dryer."

Lynda took his limp and sweaty hand and held it for a moment.

"Hi, Mr Dryer…"

"No, no, *no*, honey." He placed heavy emphasis on the final no. "It's Manny, please."

"Okay, Manny." Lynda paused. And wiped her hand along her hair, brushing it back into place. It seemed the right thing to do. "Ah… is that short for Manuel?"

"Nah. Mandezo. Mexican mother; Dutch father. I got her skin and his hair." Manny pushed his hair back. "Okay, doll-face," He turned on the couch to face Lynda. "This is the deal."

Lynda didn't know what to expect. At times like these, she always thought back to something her uncle had repeatedly said to her, which she'd carried through her entire career up to now: "Don't invite December's guests on May's turkey." In other words, don't expect too much, or you'd end up hungry at Christmas. Lynda was ready to tighten her belt.

Manny inhaled and began his shtick: "As you know, I am one of the most influential producers on the Western Seaboard."

Lynda nodded.

"And I can make or break just about anyone's career with the snap of my fingers." He snapped his fingers in front of her eyes, just to show that her how easy it was.

Lynda nodded again.

"Now, I've noticed that your ratings have been climbing up. Not like a rocket, but just enough for me to notice that they've climbed, if you catch my meaning."

Lynda nodded yet again.

Manny pointed to the table, where the three envelopes sat, heavy and bulging pregnantly in the middle. Lynda flashed a glance at the envelopes.

"In those envelopes, I have two upcoming jobs, Lynda. The one is basically doing what you're doing now, with a slight pay rise. If you walk out right now, you get it, regardless of whatever gets said between us here tonight. Hell, you deserve it. You've got that much coming to you, so I don't mind giving it to you…"

"But?" Lynda interrupted.

"But what?"

"But what about the other two envelopes?

"Aha!" Manny raised his finger. "If you didn't interrupt me, this would go a lot quicker. But now, we talk. Those other envelopes are where the conversation begins in earnest. If you don't like what I have to say, you get to take the second envelope, and walk. Consider it your separation package, if you will. But of course, we all know that the magic lies in envelope number three. As you're well aware, Lynda, my girl," he paused to look Lynda square in the eyes. "TV is the most powerful force in the world – hell, across every planet in the system. And why? Why is because it is for the people, and what the people want, they get."

Manny smoothed his hair across his head. "What was the most successful show of last season?"

That was easy; Lynda knew straight away. "*The Stars and their Bodyguards.*"

Manny nodded. "Correct. And the season before that?"

"Ah… I'm not too sure. I think it was either *Lives!* or *Who is Debby Interviewing?*"

"Yes, Lynda. Bang on the money again. It was *Lives!*, and Debby ran a close second. So, from this, what can we conclude?"

Lynda shrugged nervously.

"We can conclude that the people don't want to see movies. They don't want to see make-believe. People want to see people. That's what life stars are all about – famous people lead their lives, and we record it and give it to their masses, so that while they watch they can forget about their shitty little tenement lives and their dead-end, die-at-35-from-emphysema jobs. Lynda, everybody wants to be rich and glamorous. Everybody wants to have an apartment like this, or even bigger." Manny waved his hand around his apartment. "And in our entertainment, Lynda, we give it to them. Do you understand? But now I want you to tell me something. What about the dark side?"

"The what?" Lynda stuttered. She was a bit taken back by this fast-talking little man that had her career in the palm of his hand. Why did he have to keep asking so many questions? Why couldn't she just give him a blowjob and get her promotion, the way it was usually done? Or, even better still, just get her promotion.

"Are you listening, Lynda?"

Lynda nodded.

"Good, because this is where the crux of it comes in. You see, this is where my whole plan comes together. Out of the billions of mindless viewers who religiously turn on their sets every second of the day, how many of them out there want to be a spy, a superhero, some kind of killer on the loose? How many want to lose their inhibitions and take out their bad day at work by blowing some punk away, fucking some two-dollar whore, or beating the crap out of some pathetic-excuse-for-breathing, trash drug user because he still owes them from last week?"

Lynda eyed Manny intently.

"Did you know Lynda, that violence sells? Thirty-six-point-five percent of all people who watch the news do it only so that they can see somebody getting shot or beaten up! In the latest Fordorolla 3 litre ad, 15% of all buyers say they bought the car just because Sharaz Brightman got fucked on the hood of one in last week's episode of *Kneeburns*. Sex sells too."

Lynda had to agree. Sex did sell.

"So, what I'm saying, Lynda, is that if you can show people real sex and violence…"

"What," Lynda interrupted. "Like snuff films?" She wasn't too shocked. Entertainment was entertainment these days, and people would pay to watch just about anything.

Manny shook his head. "No. Well, sort of. More like a real-life snuff series!" He paused for a short while to compose his thoughts. "You see, it's a fact of life that there are people out there who do lead these sorts of lives, Lynda. All we have to do is find them, catch them on film, and you – Lynda Taratello – can host the show."

Her own show! Manny Dryer had just offered her her own show! Lynda paused for a moment.

"Well, ah…" How would they do it? How would they track down murderers or pimps or criminals – people who managed to do what they did by virtue of being difficult to track down?

"Aah, Lynda, I can see your mind working already: how are we going to do it? How will we find and track down our quarry, and how will we bring them to the masses?"

She nodded, and a blonde ringlet sprung from behind her ear and down the side of her face. She reached to play with it between her fingers.

Manny grinned at her. "The answer," he smiled and nodded his head like some all-knowing hippy drug guru from the 60s, "is simple. It's called the Oedipus Project."

"The what?"

Manny took another slug from his drink. "The Oedipus Project, Lynda. In Greek myth, Oedipus was the guy who killed his old man and shagged his mother – quite a kinky guy, I agree. Anyway, I don't want to get in to too much detail – most of this stuff is on a need-to-know basis – but this Oedipus Project basically gives us the technology to have a satellite track one individual through anything short of 10 miles of solid rock, and still deliver almost perfect pictures. I know it. I've seen it. All you have to do is code the thing with the vitals of your target, and it'll track them by heartbeat, heat omissions, infrared, ultraviolet, x-ray – hell, if I wanted to know how many calories he had for lunch, I could analyse the toxins in his farts! If he was looking cool, but I thought he was nervous, I could analyse the acid secretions in his sweat from 500 miles away in space!"

Manny brushed his hair back. "Now that, Lynda, my girl, is serious shit!"

Lynda sat on the couch, trying to absorb all of the information. She was interested.

"Okay, say I'm interested... who is the first target on our show?"

Manny smiled. "Leagues ahead of you, baby. I've got him already, and boy, is our first episode showing promise."

*

They sat, watching the lone man in the other corner light a cigarette and throw the crumpled, empty pack to the floor. Agent Fuchs lifted his hand to his mouth and spoke into the microphone attached to the back of his watch. His face was blank for a few short seconds as he listened to some instructions over his headset earphone. He nodded.

"Okay," Fuchs turned to Agent Heffman. "Delcaprio will be entering through the south entrance," he nodded to the front door of the shop, "in T minus..." he looked at his watch. "Eighty-five seconds, and counting. We are to support, and in the case of plan capitulation, we are to intervene. Target must be captured alive."

"Roger." Heffman nodded. They both shifted in their chairs, each of their hands dropping to the Taser guns at their belts. They were both ready for action.

Heffman nudged Fuchs with his elbow. "Here he is. He's about to make contact."

Fuchs raised his watch to his mouth. "Agent Delcaprio has entered, wearing a pink tracksuit top, red Adidas running shorts, and a pair of trainers. He is approaching the target… Bingo! Contact. Repeat: contact has been made."

Agent Delcaprio walked over to the big man in the corner with the dirty, beige great coat and tousled, dark hair. Holloway?"

Jim nodded. "Delcaprio?"

Agent Delcaprio pushed his running hood back and slid into the booth. He waved at a passing waitress. "I'll have a soda and lime, thanks."

The agent turned his moustachioed face to Jim. "Holloway, I think I've got what you might be looking for." Delcaprio lifted his left hand out of the pouch on the front of his tracksuit top. He left a small, newspaper-wrapped parcel on the table.

"And your right hand?"

Delcaprio frowned. "What about my right hand? What you talking about, James? Don't you trust me?"

Jim leant forward, his face closing the gap between them. Delcaprio could smell the burger on his breath.

"You've got your right hand under the table," Jim said evenly. "I don't know what you've got your finger on, but I've got my hand under the table, and I've got my finger on the trigger of my gun. At this range, I'll blow your stomach through your chair and all over that bitch eating spaghetti at the table across the room."

"Hey man…" Delcaprio began to protest.

"Shut it, you stupid secret-agent fuck." Jim was starting to get pissed. He had said hello. He had been nice. And now he felt his temper flair.

"Listen, man, don't do anything nervy. Everybody's cool…" Delcaprio was starting to panic. He inched his right hand closer to the Taser strapped under his shirt.

Jim gritted his teeth. He felt the blood throb through his temples and his temperature started to rise.

"Aagh, fuck!" Jim snapped.

The boom of his gun splattering Agent Delcaprio all over the booth seemed to plunge the café into an underwater, slow-motion world.

Jim pumped another shell into Delcaprio's chest, and jumped clear of the table, his long coat flapping and unfurling about him. Some women screamed, and people were diving for the floor. As he landed, Jim rolled and turned to face agents Heffman and Fuchs. They probably thought that everybody talked into their hands, had crewcuts, and boasted Taser-sized bulges in their jackets. Idiots.

Heffman scrambled out his Taser, and Jim churned three shells towards him. One of them caught him in the shoulder, and Heffman spun towards the ground, squirting a red circle of blood across the tiled floor. Fuchs dived over his chair and tumbled for cover behind a large pot plant containing a plastic rose bush.

Jim stood up and ran towards the agents.

A man jumped up and tried to run – to where, only God knew. Jim bulldozed him out the way and charged the agents down. Heffman squeezed off two Taser shells. Fuchs shot out a half a dozen rounds at Jim. Two of them came mighty close. Jim blew Heffman away, his head popping like a soft, ripe fruit. Fuchs tried another two shots at Jim, but they missed. Jim reached the pot plant and dived over, his body hurtled through the stems and leaves, and he got caught in the face by a plastic thorn.

Fuchs and Holloway rolled on the ground, trading blows and struggling. People ran across the café. Women screamed. Men shouted.

Suddenly, Jim jerked free from Fuchs, his left hand latched tight around the agent's throat, and he pounded his gun into Fuchs's skull. Fuchs's head snapped back onto the floor, and Jim pumped his fist into Fuchs's face, turning it into a bloody mass. Fuchs lay still. Jim stopped and stood up. He hoisted Fuchs's limp body by the lapel and slung him over his shoulder.

On the way out, Jim reached into his pocket, pulled out some change and loose notes, and threw them onto the table.

*

The light of a pale, mid-afternoon sun on a cloudy day shone onto the purple, swelling mass that was the face of Special Agent Ernst Fuchs. A glass of warm water splashed him; he moved his head and tried to open his eyes, but they stayed puffed and swollen shut. Jim Holloway grabbed him by the hair.

"Okay, Agent…" he stopped to read Fuch's badge. "…Fuchs. My name is Jim Holloway, but you probably know that. You probably also know that I have a reputation for being a violent man. On the other hand, I think I'm a reasonable sort of guy, really. Now I'm going to leave you for a short while to grab myself a cup of coffee. While I'm gone, I want you to think about a few things. I want you to think of yourself tied up here on the chair. I want you to think of your happy family whose photographs you have in your wallet – nice pictures, by the way – and finally, I want you to think of what you're going to say to me when I get back later on. Okay?"

Jim patted Fuchs on the cheek. The agent squirmed against the cuffs (his own) that secured him to the chair.

"You fuck, Holloway! You stupid fuck! You're going to die, you know that! They'll come for me…"

Jim turned and walked out the room. "Yeah, right. Sticks and stones… See you later, Fuchs."

*

Johnny Centauri was pissed off when he stormed through his apartment door.

"Okay, Jim, you better tell me what the fuck's going on. I heard bad things from a very reliable source. From what I can tell, you blew a whole herd of agents away in some food joint and Mayor Krupses is moving heaven and earth to make sure that you're caught and your ass is nailed to the wall."

Jim shrugged. "Have some coffee, John. Let me say my piece."

"Fuck that, Jim! I don't want coffee. I want to know what's going on."

Jim felt particularly calm. "Yeah, John. Well, so do I. But I've got somebody in the back room who can help us answer these questions."

"What?" John ran across to the kitchen counter and threw a coffee mug against the wall. "You've got somebody *here*? Who? From where? Fuck, Jim! You can't act like this! This isn't the fucking Stone Age." John ran his fingers through his hair as he paced up and down the living room. "Okay, Jim. Explain quick, because I'm fucked off. And you don't want that."

Jim leant back in his chair, placed his hands behind his head, and put his feet up on the coffee table. He looked at Johnny Centauri.

"So?"

Johnny looked back. "So? What do you mean, 'so'? So what?"

"So, are you finished making a noise like a chicken with its fucking head chopped off?"

"Jim, you exasperating cunt! A chicken with no head can't make any noise, because its got no head."

Jim waved his hand in front of his face. "Oh, well, fuck. You know what I mean. Are you ready to listen?"

"Yah," John stopped pacing and sat down back in his chair. He started tapping his foot. "Okay, Jim. Fire away. I'm listening."

Jim leant forward in his chair. "Well, John, after I left you at the takeaway, I phoned the nearest government agency department – they're listed in the book – and I gave them the contact number that the grey man who hired me told me to give when I had any information. Anyway, they put this Delcaprio guy on the line, and I told him that I thought there was some involvement from his side of the fence and that maybe this Isabella Carla had help from a source on the inside…"

"Well, why did you say that?"

Jim shrugged. "It was just a feeling I had. Besides, there was that ID. Also, there was the file they gave me when I started the job. It looks too set up. She had a file that read like a handbook on how to be a career criminal. There was way too much detail. I mean, she's supposed to have committed all these crimes, right? But she's never been taken into custody once, and yet they've got all of her background details?" Jim shrugged again. "I don't know, John. It sounded like a heap of shit to me, but I took it. At least the money was good. Besides, I had nothing else to do."

"Okay, fine, Jim. So what happened?"

"This Delcaprio guy arranged a meeting with me at this café, The Brazilio, and I get there and he's got two goons shadowing me from the corner. Then he arrives, and he tries to slip me a parcel with the one hand, meanwhile he's got the other hand under the table, trying to sneak his Taser up on me. So I blew him away, killed one of thee goons, and took this one –" he thumbed over his shoulder towards the bedroom – "hostage, so he could help me sort this mess out."

"Okay," Johnny nodded. "Fair enough, Jim. But couldn't you have just run out of the place? Don't you think that killing them was a bit out of hand?"

Jim shook his head. "No, Johnny. These guys were after me. It was me or them – you know how it goes. It turned out to be them."

"So, Jim?" Johnny put his fists on his hips. "What now? Every agent this side of Agora knows where I live, and by now, they'd know about you and me." He lifted his hand and looked to his watch. "I give them 15 minutes, maybe less."

*

Pain is a transitory thing. You get hit, you hurt, and then it goes away. Sometimes you get hit, you hurt, and then you die – but then it doesn't matter, because you're dead anyway. Of course, there are different types of pain. There is the pain of getting hurt on the inside, and sometimes that takes longer to heal than the pain on the outside.

Jim knew about the pain on the inside. When you sink into a sea of loneliness, then you know that you're in pain on the inside. When your life revolves around something that isn't there anymore, then it's a sure thing that you're in pain on the inside.

And Jim was buggered if he knew how to heal that sort of hurt.

Sure, it didn't hurt like it used to. It wasn't so sharp anymore; now it was a dull throb. But it was still there – always there, like the memory of your first dog.

And suddenly, this warm woman, this smell, this texture, this feeling, this knowledge of beauty – she bought all the hurt back to him. And she healed it. Jim had never known anyone like her. In fact, he had never even known her – but the fact that she was out there, and that he had met her, gave him hope. When he thought about her, the fog in his head cleared and the fucking steel cage around his heart loosened slightly. Jim believed that with her he could be the man he'd always wanted to be.

He could be funny and caring; strong, yet sensitive. He could come home from work and tell her that he'd had the sort of day that made him proud to bring their children into the world. He'd had a day filled with hope. And...

The sharp knocking on the bathroom door woke Jim up.

"Jim? Jim, you alright in there?"

Jim shook his head clear. He felt like shit. He had a cut across his face from his fight with the agents and he wanted to curl up and go back to sleep where the grass was right, the cows were right, and none of the complicated sort of shit that happened in real life happened.

"Jim!" Johnny shouted again, this time banging on the door a bit harder. "Jim, you okay?"

"Yah," Jim called back. "I'm hundreds. Just fell asleep, that's all."

"Okay. Well, are you coming out now?"

"Yeah, right now. Lemme just sort out the paperwork, you know what I mean?"

"Okay. I'll see you now."

Jim finished with the toilet and washed his hands and face. He looked at himself in the mirror. He wasn't looking his best. It wasn't that he looked like shit (because he always looked like shit); it was that he *felt* like shit. Usually he was numb to feelings, but now he was feeling all sorts of things. It was one of those pain-on-the-inside things – the sort of pain where cows where always on the other side of the fence and they were always eating amazingly green grass, no matter what happened. And he could never get there, no matter how hard he tried. No matter how hard he needed to.

Jim turned to the door, about to return to the living room, when he heard the click. He stopped, and he knew. It was the click of somebody knocking the safety off their pistol. The sound could have been one of a million things, but not now, not today. Not in Johnny Centauri's apartment. Jim knew that when he walked out of the toilet, he would be walking into a world of pain. That would be a good title for a country and western song, he thought: "Out of the Toilet And Into the Pain".

Jim grinned to himself. He wondered whether Johnny had been with them all along, or if he had turned just now. He wondered what was in it for Johnny. And he resolved then and there how he was going to kill the man who'd once been his friend, who'd once been his enemy, who was then his friend again, and now was his enemy again. Fuck me, but life was complicated, he mused.

Jim sidled up next to the door and dropped to one knee.

"Johnny," he called out.

"Yeah, Jim? What's it?"

Jim smiled. "I'm outta paper. Can you bring me some?"

"Aah, for fuck's sake, Jim. There's some in the cupboard

under the sink."

"Nah, I checked that already. Fucking thing's empty."

Jim could almost hear the cogs turning in Johnny's mind. "Ah, okay, Jim," he replied. "I've got no more. Can't you just leave it and come out of the fucking toilet? Take a good shower later on, for Christ's sake."

Jim delivered his *coup de grace*: "Listen John, if you don't bring me the fucking newspaper or something, I'm gonna wipe my ass on your expensive, monogrammed, fucking silver-spoon-in-my-mouth, Turkish cotton, 600-thread-count, goddamned shaggy white bath towels. You understand me?"

There was a small pause.

Suddenly, the door burst open and the toilet exploded in a cascade of water and ceramic chunks as two high-velocity rounds ripped apart where Jim would have been sitting if he had still been on the toilet.

Just as suddenly, there was a boom and a splat, and the sound of a body falling to the floor. That quickly, Johnny Centauri was dead.

Jim stood up from where he'd been kneeling by the door and looked down at the body. The body was all he *could* look at, because the head had been blown almost entirely off. Jim's bullet had entered under the jaw, and exploded out the back of the head, taking most of the brain and skull with it. The lounge would need a clean-up.

Jim startled rifling through John's pockets and pulled out a card that seemed out of place from the others:

Special Agent Petra Verkayik

Alpha Prime Intelligence Agency

51 Dazzle Street

QWE 737 1451

Interesting.

"Hey, Mister Secret Agent Man," Jim walked through to the room where Agent Fuchs was tied up. "Explain this to me and maybe I won't throw you out of the window…"

*

CHAPTER 5:
THE MOUSE IN
THE HOUSE

Senator Hymes wore a very dark and very well-cut suit that fitted him like a soft, sleek glove. He was a very good-looking man: tall and imperious, broad shouldered, temples slightly greying, piercing blue eyes beneath a dark, strong set of brows. He was not so much good looking, as ideal looking. In fact, he was perhaps a little too good looking to be a senator. But he was a senator, and a good one at that.

The free people of Alpha City – and the other three cities (Bora, Central and Gaia) that comprised the populous holdings of Alpha Prime – looked to Senator Hymes for their political lead. He was their elected leader and citizen number one. At the moment, he sat in a small room in which the walls and floor joined seamlessly. A table flowed up out of the floor – a smooth, liquid column that mushroomed into an oval tabletop and flattened itself between the three men in the room, in the same pristine white as the walls and floor.

There were two other men in the room. One wore a grey suit and had dead, expressionless eyes; the other wore a navy-blue suit with military insignia adorning his shoulders and chest. He had a walrus moustache.

"General Abhakar," Senator Hymes addressed the walrus, who nodded. "Mr Simione," he turned to the second guest, whose shaved head mirrored the motion.

Hymes shivered. Simione always reminded him of a shark. And Hymes felt like the shark's next meal. But not this time. Not this time, Simione, you mysterious grey fuck. I've got you now.

"Gentlemen, I've called you here today because it seems that one – or possibly both – of you, has been pissing in my garden." Hymes slammed his fist onto the table. "And today it stops. Here and now."

Simione's face was unchanged and expressionless as always; Abhakar was silent, but his eye started to twitch. A small tic beneath his right eye, but Hymes saw it.

Hymes pulled a folder out of his briefcase and threw it onto the table, its contents sprawling across the smooth, white plastic surface.

"I want to know about the Oedipus Project, and I want to know *now*. I want to know about Project Pandora, and I want to know *now*. And lastly, I want to know about this man" – he pointed at a wall and on it appeared an image of a pale, skinny man with gold chains – "Mandezo, otherwise known as Manny Dryer."

The senator leant forward and placed both of his hands firmly on the table. He looked at the other two men with ill-concealed contempt. "I'm waiting."

General Abhakar cleared his throat. "Richard," he addressed the senator with a small nod of his head. "Of these things I know nothing. I deal purely with the military wings – you know that. However, I'm not certain that Simione over here can say the same."

Simione sat motionless for a while, looking at the

pyramid of his ten fingertips touching in front of his chest. He did not look up as he spoke, his voice slithering out of his throat, slow, thick, and accented. "Tell me, senator, how you got your information. If I am your information wing, tell me how you got your information without me knowing about it?"

The senator held up his hand. "I have my sources, Simione. You don't think I trust you enough to leave intelligence entirely in your hands, do you?"

Simione shook his head, smiling to himself. "No, I suppose not." He hadn't credited the senator with such shrewdness. It was a mistake he would not make again. Before he spoke, he waited for a while, filling the gap between the two men with a heavy, curdling silence.

"Okay, senator. I'll tell you about the Oedipus Project, Project Pandora, and Manny Dryer. It's too late for you to do anything about it anyway." Simione smiled up at Hymes. It was a cold and thin-lipped grin, exposing a full set of trim, white teeth. Definitely like a shark.

"The Oedipus Project is now complete. The project concerned the construction of a very sophisticated satellite – probably the most advanced surveillance satellite known to man. Project Pandora was not initially our project; it was started by Galactic Infiltration – their attempt at the ultimate human weapon – but stopped due to lack of funding. We found a sponsor, took the project over, and here we are today."

"And Manny Dryer?"

"He sponsored the Oedipus Project – got all the right people at the right networks to make the right noises. He sponsored the Pandora Project, too."

"And what does he have to gain from all this?"

"Oh, you mean apart from having Alpha Prime's

intelligence agency as his friends?" Simione smirked. "He gains the most important thing in a modern society: ratings, of course, good senator. Ratings."

Simione reached into his coat, and pulled out a small, silver play-disc. "You should watch your TV more often." He slid the disc over the table towards Hymes. "This was the pilot episode on channel 183. It aired last Friday night at midnight. It'll be on channels 170 through 190 tomorrow night. If the next episode is as good as this, then I think it will be on many more channels before the show is through."

The senator made a small, grunting noise as he picked up the play-disc. "What is this show called, Simione?"

Simione displayed his biggest and sharkiest grin so far. "*Guns and Broads*, senator," he said. "The show is called *Guns and Broads*!"

*

Petra Verkayik was a thin mouse of a woman in a small, grey suit, with her hair pulled behind her head in a tight, neat bun, and her glasses perched smartly on her small, mousey nose. She looked, Jim thought, as mouselike as a human could possibly get.

"Jim Holloway?" she said.

Jim's eyes opened in shock as she spoke. He realised he had been expecting her to squeak.

He regained his composure. "Yah, that's me."

"Do you realise that half of Alpha City is looking for you? In fact, some grey men are probably on their way over here, now, even as we speak."

In his head, Jim thought she said "squeak" instead of "speak". He grinned. "Well, you know, mouse girl, there's nothing I can do about that. Agents will…"

"I'm sorry?" The small woman looked up at Jim with a quizzical expression. "What did you just call me?"

"Ahh…" Honestly, Jim couldn't remember calling her anything.

"You called me 'mouse girl'!" she said indignantly.

"Shit!" said Jim. "Sorry. I'm a little unstable right now. I'm not thinking as straight as I normally do. My emotions are a bit giddy; I think there's something wrong with me, and I think it's got something to do with somebody I'm looking for."

Petra Verkayik shook her head. "I can't believe you called me 'mouse girl'."

"Aw fuck, get over yourself!" Suddenly his temper burned bright as a napalm flame and he reached across her desk and lifted her out of her seat by her lapels. He wanted to crush her mousey neck in his thick fingers and then shoot her in her mousey face.

She smelt so nice and clean.

That made him sad, and he let her go. She flopped onto her desk. She was so clean, and neat, and good smelling. He couldn't kill her. Jim pictured her dead little mousey body on the floor, the back of her head spread across the floor, and her neat little bun at the back of her head mingled with pink brain Her glasses on the tiled floor, broken. He pictured her poor little mousey mother and father at her funeral in Mouseville. It was all so pathetic and sad.

Now Jim wanted to cry. And he did – one lone tear at first, and then another, followed by its friends.

A few moments later, mouse girl handed Jim a tissue.

"Thank you," he said politely.

"Um, Mr Holloway," she began timidly. She moved over to sit next to Jim, and put her small arm around his enormous frame. "Is there anything you want to tell me?"

"Yes," Jim sobbed, nodding his head. He took a deep, shuddering breath. "There's a nightclub in Emera City called The Grind," he began. And he carried on. He told her everything. About the gut wound. About Johnny. About Isabella Carla, the dreams, his history. Every damn thing that had happened to him over the last few days. He even told her about the cows that ate grass, and that pinged in his head.

She listened silently. When he was finished, she got up and moved back behind her desk. She sat down and punched the keyboard for a few seconds, then spun her screen around to face Jim.

"I think I know why you're cracking up, Mr Holloway."

"Jim," Jim insisted.

"Okay, Jim." She began again. "I think I could know why you're having these problems. Take a look at the screen."

Jim looked. It was a progress report of her latest case. It concerned the disappearance of a government agent, Kurt Spack – a grey suit. Jim scanned the text: Spack had carried out a standard mission on Epiphany, a small moon off Bilara, one of the rim planets. Within a week of returning, he began showing signs of irregular behaviour and erratic thought processes. A little over two weeks later, he jumped out of his office on the 35th floor, and landed on a car only five storeys into his fall. He survived – injured, but alive – but he was never seen again. Somebody had made off with him, and she needed to solve the mystery. Up till now, she had had very little to go on. Up till now.

"Tell me, Jim," said the mousey agent. "Does your dream girl look anything like this?" She tapped her keyboard and a picture of Isabella Carla came onto the screen.

Jim felt his heart skip a beat. He couldn't do anything but

stare at the picture before him.

"Yes," mouse girl mouthed sarcastically at Jim's reaction. "I think she does."

Jim composed himself. "Okay, Petra, so it seems as though we're kinda on the same team for the time being. You're looking for Spack, who is looking for our dream girl; and I'm looking for dream girl. I think we're both looking for the same thing here. The only question I need answered from you is: what was your card doing in Johnny Centauri's wallet?"

The special agent shrugged her petite shoulders. "He's the best manhunter in the city. I'm looking for a man…"

"With blonde hair and a tan?" Jim interjected, smiling at his own joke.

Petra looked at him levelly. "I'm looking for Spack."

"I know that. It was just a line from an old movie. It was a joke, but you missed it."

"Sorry," said Petra. "I try not to have a sense of humour at work. It can be risky."

"Yeah, I know what you mean. One day you might laugh and your head'll fall off."

"Up yours."

Jim nodded his head. "Exactly. But enough of this charming banter. Do you know if Johnny ever found anything?"

"He *said* he had something. A lead of sorts. But then you landed on the scene, and I stopped hearing from him."

"Well, you probably won't be hearing from him again."

"How do you know this?" Petra was concerned.

Jim placed his fingertips together in what he hoped was a sagely pose. "I have my ways. Also, I blew his head off in his apartment."

"What? Are you insane?" Petra jumped up from her seat.

Jim shrugged and smiled.

Petra's small eyes widened. "Are you seriously telling me… I… I mean… you just killed…"

"Yes, that's right." Jim stood, hoisted his coat from the back of his chair, put it on, and walked towards the door. In the doorway, he paused. "I've got the key to his apartment. I'm heading there now to go through his case files. You coming?"

He turned and walked out.

"Yes! Wait!" Petra shrieked. "Just hold on, let me get my coat. I'm coming."

*

Petra retched again and threw up into the kitchen sink.

Jim chuckled. "Alright, baby. Puke it all up. Besides, your ass clenches when you hurl, and it looks quite good from where I'm sitting." He laughed some more.

A small, mousey hand thrust out behind her and raised its middle finger at Jim, but he didn't see it because he had already turned to Johnny's case files. He had the file he wanted in his hand. It seemed that, through a nursing friend of his, Johnny had tracked down Agent Spack to a medical establishment designed for patients with special psychological needs. A nuthouse, in other words. The Nupierre Medical Institute. He read through the rest of the file.

"Christ, you could've at least cleaned up a little." Petra wiped her chin as she turned from the sink.

"What for?" said Jim mildly. "Johnny isn't complaining. Besides, we're leaving now anyway." He stood up and stretched his fingers out in front of him, cracking his knuckles. "You ready?"

"What?" the petite agent was incredulous. "We just got here. You can't just charge off! We have to examine the evidence. Check with our sources, verify our leads…"

A groaning from the spare room stopped her dead in her tracks.

"What the hell?" she whipped a gun out from behind her back. It was small and sleek and shiny, and looked like the kind of gun a sexy little white mouse with pretty pink ears and silk lingerie would have strapped to the inside of her thigh.

"Ah, that's nothing," Jim said, waving dismissively at the bedroom door. "It's just one of the agents I picked up at the café. Don't worry about him. He'll be fine."

"Oh." Petra's face went blank for a moment. She took a moment to think. "Jim, do you realise that since this case started, you've killed at least nine people, and captured and kidnapped one more? This includes the deaths of two agents, and your oldest friend."

"Yeah?" Jim shrugged. "What's your point?"

Petra gestured awkwardly with her hands. "Don't you have any respect for human life? And not even other people's – I mean, how about your own life, for a start? You're an emotional wreck, you look as though you haven't slept in two days, changed clothes in three, or eaten a healthy meal in about two months! And then there's the way you interact with other people. You can't just charge into a place and shoot everyone until somebody tells you what you want, and then leave that mess behind you. Jim, there's more to life than just being tough!"

Jim nodded. "Great. You ready to go, now? We're off to the Nupierre Institute. And this time, I've got a plan."

Petra perked up. "That's better. What is it?"

Jim grinned. "Charge in and shoot everyone until

somebody tells me what I want to hear!"

"Aaarrggh!" Petra balled her fists and her whole body stiffened. "You are the most frustrating and insane person I have ever met in my life!"

"Come on," Jim rejoined. "Last one to the elevator is a rotten egg." He turned and darted his overweight body out through the door and into the lobby.

*

The taxi stopped outside the Nupierre institute. His name was Zephadene, and he had a Moroccan accent. He had refused to give them a ride any further after Jim had called him Ephadrene, and had mocked his accent for five minutes. Android mechanisms did have feelings too, it appeared, and it was only after Petra had shut Jim up and soothed the cab with promises of return fares and double payments, that the taxi finally consented to transport them to their destination.

The walls surrounding the institute were a creamy, yellow colour, 12 foot high, and were mounted with cameras and razor wire. They ran in either direction for what seemed like a very long way indeed. It was a big place.

Jim walked up to the gates – massive, grey, steel palisade affairs – and called to the security guard on the other side. "Hey, busboy!"

The security guard, resplendent in an excessively neat uniform – black, fringed with yellow – walked over to the gate. His nametag was gold with black, embossed lettering, and it looked like he had used a spirit level to place it on his chest pocket. Probably the same spirit level he had used to trim either side of his moustache. The tag read "Vance".

"Sir?" he enquired of Jim with a slight incline of his head

(15 degrees, no more).

"Vance," said Jim, glancing at the nametag. "I am looking for a friend of mine whom I believe is interred in this facility. If I give you his name, may I go and see him?" Jim paused. "Please?"

"I am afraid not, sir." Vance spoke with genuine compassion. "This is a restricted facility. Only those with the correct credentials are permitted entry."

"Oh, really?" Jim started to become agitated. He had been nice. He had used his manners. Fuck, he had even bothered to read this guy's stupid, phony-gold nametag and address him by name, and now the dipstick wasn't going to let him in?

Jim slapped his hand against his chest. "Well, I've got credentials." He reached down for his holster to pull out his guns. This neat fuck would let him in, or he would die with a neat hole right through his neat head.

Petra put a hand on Jim's shoulder and cleared her throat loudly.

"Sorry – Vance, was it?"

"Yes, ma'am." The 15-degree nod.

"What my colleague here is trying to say is that we are looking for a suspect in a case of ours, and we believe that he may be inside." She whipped out her agency ID badge and presented it to the guard. "Here are my credentials."

Vance studied the badge, and then raised his hand to his head in a small, precise salute. "My apologies, Special Agent Verkayik. I will open up for you and your partner right away." He returned to his cubicle to open the gate.

Petra grabbed Jim by the arm. "You were going to kill him, weren't you?" she whispered fiercely into his ear. "I saw the look in your face. If he didn't open the gate, you would have shot him, wouldn't you?"

"Nah," muttered Jim unconvincingly. "Maybe I would've just winged him. Throw a little scare into him, that sort of thing. Nothing serious."

The enormous gates opened, and they walked into the institute grounds.

Jim turned to Petra. "Okay, Miss Special Secret Agent with flashy credentials. Now what?"

"Now we show the main desk Agent Spack's picture, and ask if they can take us to him."

"That's a good plan," Jim admitted.

*

Agent Spack was a thin man, who had once packed muscle tightly onto his body, but was now beginning to lose shape. His skin sagged in places. He had droopy eyes, and wide tracts of grey running through his long, spiky hair. He needed a haircut and a shave. He also needed to commit suicide.

Jim knew the look.

"Spack, I'm Holloway. This here is Special Agent Verkayik. We're looking for some information on a woman, and we think you may be able to help us."

Agent Spack raised one eyebrow at the pair standing in front of him. They certainly were an odd couple: a fat, out-of-shape jock with heavy jowls, whiskey breath, and an overcoat more crumpled than a bum's brown paper bag, and a spunky little agent with her neat glasses perched on the edge of her nose in a sexy, young schoolteacher kind of way.

The old agent peered for a while at the fat one, and then he burst out laughing. Agent Kurt Spack raised his finger to point at Jim.

"You, too!"

Jim looked at him quizzically.

"Don't play dumb with me, Hollowhead, or whatever your name is. She's got you as well, hasn't she? I recognise the look, because I see it every time I look in the mirror. Have you tried to off yourself, or hasn't it got that bad yet?"

Jim didn't move.

Agent Spack chuckled. "Don't worry, it will."

Petra began to speak, but Jim interrupted: "Listen up, spamball. You can strangle yourself with your mommy's pantyhose for all I care. That's why you're in the nuthouse – because you are a NUT! I just want to know if you have any info on this lady."

Jim pulled out the picture of Isabella Carla.

Agent Spack glanced at the picture, then sat silent for a moment before he spoke again. "You know, before they locked me up here, I was a good agent. One of the best, in fact. I had 20 years of distinguished service. And if there's one thing I know, it's how to track somebody down."

"So?" interrupted Jim.

"So, what I'm trying to say," Spack went on calmly, "is that I know how to track down our girl. But I'll only tell you if you get me out of here."

"And what if I blow you away right now because you didn't tell me what I wanted to hear?" said Jim.

Spack shrugged, cool as a cucumber. "You'll be doing me a favour. I'm in here because I tried to kill myself in the first place, don't forget. She is the only reason I have to live. If I can't have her, then I might as well as die now anyway."

"But getting you out of here will take time," Petra began. "There's paperwork, and…"

Kurt interrupted. "Grow up, agent! Do you think I'm ever getting out of this place? Do you think they'll ever let me go after they've picked my brain apart and got what they want? I either die here, or you take me now and I lead you to the girl."

"Okay," said Jim. "One more question. And if I like your answer, then we have a deal. If not, then I leave you here to rot. If you knew where Isabella Carla was, then why did you jump out of the window instead of tracking her down?"

Agent Spack was amused. Jim was sharper than he looked. Spack reached over to his bedside table and pulled out a small, plastic bottle containing some pink tablets. "Because I didn't have these." He tossed the bottle to Jim, who caught it in a meaty hand. "They take the edge off a bit, and help me to think of anything besides her. If I don't have one every few hours, I begin to look for the highest ledge around. They keep me sane. Or, at least, marginally so."

Jim poured a few of the tablets into his pocket, and threw the container back to Spack.

Jim looked at Petra. "I don't like drugs, but I'll keep some just in case. You never know." He turned back to Spack. "Right, let's get you out of these straps; We're busting you out of this joint." He smiled his distinctly Jim smile. "Let's crack this nut out of his shell!"

And then he burst out laughing.

*

Sitting in the taxi Zephadene on the promised return leg at double price, one mile over the streets of Alpha City, the wind whipped around the inside of the cab, just before Jim shut the door. Then he looked through the window and saw the body of Agent Spack hurtle through the air, spinning limply on its trajectory to the ground. The gaping hole in Spack's chest seemed to change size as his body spun and flipped towards the oblivious citizens below. Very soon, Jim lost sight of the body through the smog and the growing distance. Now he turned to Agent Petra Verkayik.

She lay next to him in the back of the cab, her body stiff as a board after one of the nurses had shot her with a paralysis dart, usually reserved for the more unruly patients. She was totally conscious, but would have no control over any motor function of her body for at least another 40 minutes. She was supine, had a pulse and couldn't talk –almost the ideal woman, Jim grinned to himself.

Just for kicks, he pulled a cigarette out of his crumpled pack and stuck one of them, butt end first, up her left nostril. He could see that she hated it, but she couldn't squirm, or squeal, or protest. Jim cackled out loud, and then leant back in his seat. He cast his mind back to the recent events at the Nupierre Institute.

After they had freed Spack, they'd made their way to the end of the ward, where an orderly had asked what exactly they thought they were doing. Petra had explained that Spack was wanted for questioning, and she'd flashed her badge, but the intern wasn't buying any, and slapped the red alarm button. That was more or less when Jim had lost control.

He'd pumped two slugs into the orderly's chest, then grabbed the body and hurled it under the thick, steel door that was sliding out of the roof to isolate the ward. Once the door was jammed by the orderly's body, Jim and the agents had slid under it, only to find that there were three security guards waiting for them, along with two male nurses with dart guns. One of them had caught Petra square in the shoulder with a paralysis dart. Jim had killed two of the guards and one of the nurses, but the other two had escaped.

By the time the three escapees had made it down to the foyer, a security team had assembled there. During a heavy gunfight, Jim had grabbed the duty matron (a skinny, old duck with grey hair) and, using her as a hostage, he'd managed to make it most of the way towards the front doors.

Most of the way.

With one eye on a crazy and still-drugged Spack, and one on his attackers – with a rapidly paralysing Petra dangled over his left shoulder, and his right arm wrapped around the elderly matron – with a gun in each hand and bullets flying around him like crazy, Jim had had far too much to concentrate on. His gun had gone off by accident, and blew the matron's head clean off her neck. The head had flown almost two yards into the air before splattering onto the floor. Jim felt shit about that. He distinctly remembered apologising.

"Oops, fuck, sorry," had been his exact words.

In the ensuing barrage of fire, Spack had caught a round in the leg. Jim had scooped the hollering, blaspheming Spack over his right shoulder, and, charging like a linebacker on horse steroids, he'd somehow managed to clear the front doors and make it out into the grounds. He'd shot the security guard in the guardhouse at the gate (unfortunately, it wasn't Vance), slammed the button to open the big, steel gate, and just as he was jogging through it to escape, he'd heard a noise behind him.

Jim had turned and looked. It was a fateful error. It was Vance, stepping out from behind a tree, with a shotgun. He'd fired a round at Jim, and it hit him right in the chest. Or, at least, right in Agent Spack's back, which was shielding his chest. Jim had squeezed off a burst of bullets at the neat-freak security guard, but Vance had already ducked back into the trees. Jim had slipped through the gates, and into their waiting cab.

The rest, as they say, was history. Except for one thing. Except for the fact that, as Spack was dying, he'd told Jim what he had found out about Isabella Carla. That she was military trained, but that her training had been funded by one of the most influential organisations in the galaxy: one of the broadcasting networks. That he had tracked it down to C… B… and then Spack had died. The useless son of a bitch.

Jim thought about this as the taxicab hummed its warm and steady way to the spaceport. There were about 30 broadcasting networks that began with the initials CB. He could name at least 12. Although, that said, there were probably only five that were powerful enough to arrange a military piece like Carla. Four of them were based in Central City, and so it was there that he had decided to go. He and Special Agent Petra Verkayik, whom, he had to admit, he was beginning to get rather fond of. She had almost survived an entire day of Jim Holloway at full tilt, and that was something. Not many people had done that, and surviving was a good prerequisite for a relationship. Well, it was a start, at any rate.

By the time they got to the spaceport, Petra had begun to recover. She still couldn't use her arms properly, but had shaken the cigarette out of her nose. It had taken her five full minutes and Jim had almost pissed himself laughing. He half dragged, half carried Petra to the check-in counter and, using her special agent pass, secured them first-class seats on a non-stop shuttle direct to Central City. It was very expensive, and of course directly against strict agency regulations, but Jim figured that he wasn't an agent, so up theirs.

He and Petra got their own cabin on board a Lex VI class cruiser, which in itself was a comment on how much the agency had paid for the flight. The Lex VI was the latest in space travel, and Jim had only ever been on a Lex III before. In a place where air travel was as cheap as a good takeaway, this shuttle trip had probably cost him a month's salary. Or cost the agency that, at least.

Jim settled down on a red, velvet chaise lounge, and put his drink back onto the automatic little drinks mat that hovered next to his hand. He pulled a blanket out from underneath him and covered himself from chest to toe. Relaxed, finally comfortable, he closed his eyes and slept.

Jim dreamt of cows. They grazed in a field of grey grass, dotted with flowers that resembled the face of the matron whose head he had shot off at Nupierre. One of the flowers opened her mouth, and out ran a squadron of lingerie-clad mice with guns, cute glasses resting on the edges of their pink noses. For some reason, that disturbed him.

Then he left the field, and saw a massive barn. A line of hundreds of cows walked in one end and out the other. Inside, Isabella Carla was milking the cows, pulling on their teats with her hands in a most suggestive manner. Jim liked that.

Above them, a TV camera hovered in the sky, recording his every movement. He reached into his holster and pulled out his gun. Aiming at the camera, he pulled back the hammer, and it clicked loudly.

Too loudly.

He opened his eyes, and realised that he was staring down the barrel of one of his own weapons. He could see that the safety was off, and that the hammer was cocked. Fury burning in her eyes, Petra Verkayik stood over him, the gun shaking in her hands.

"Jim, you fuck!" Spittle flew out the side of her mouth. "Do you like how this feels, huh? How many people did you kill back at the institute? You maniac! And what about Spack? You just tossed him out of the cab like he was some kind of trash! You almost got me killed! And then there's this cabin – my CO will go through the roof when he gets this bill! He'll probably kill me! That's if I survive another day with you!"

Insane with anger, Petra waved the gun around, and then threw it at Jim's chest, slapped him across the head, and kicked a hole through the door of the cupboard in the corner of the cabin.

She's cute when she's mad, Jim thought. "Hey, girl, take it easy. That's some temper you've got there."

"Me?!" Petra leant forward for emphasis. "Me? *I've* got some temper? What about you, Mr Mass Murderer? 'I just kill people because they piss me off!' Hah! You can take your temper and shove it where the sun don't shine, because I have had enough. From now on, we do things by the book, or we don't do them at all. Understand?" She was now pacing the small cabin. "Yes. From now on, it's my way, or the highway – is that clear? Up yours, and your fucking crazy kill-a-thon."

She stopped, grabbed Jim by the lapel, and looked him right in the eye, her face only inches away. "How many people have to die, you fat fuck? How many more until you are happy? Until we can all just go home and live a peaceful life and eat breakfast in the mornings and not have to kill anyone because the coffee was cold, and... and... oh, fuck!" And then she burst into tears.

Jim sat up and wrapped her in a blanket. He felt bad. Not for killing so many people – he justified that by telling himself that if they would leave him alone, then he'd leave them alone. The problem was that they could never just leave him alone. If he had his way, he'd leave the whole human race alone, and they could leave him in peace. Some place nice and quiet, with sunny skies and thick, green grass, and a white picket fence. But no, that would never be. So he had to go around making pretty ladies like the nice Miss Petra Verkayik upset, watching their neat little hair buns unravel and fall in brown waves that framed her sweet, sad face, tears dropping onto her perfect skin from her pointy little nose.

Jim realised that he didn't like what it felt like making this woman unhappy. And for the first time in as long as he could remember, Jim Holloway thought about somebody else. He put an arm around the now sniffling Petra, and she leant her slender body into him. She nestled against his broad chest.

"I'm sorry, Petra. I truly am sorry." Jim truly was sorry. "It feels like death and hate are all I know anymore. I've killed for so long, I think I've just forgotten how to live. I don't have a life. I don't go out for dinner, like other people, or go and watch movies. I don't have friends, or exercise, apart from on the shooting range. For years now, my life has been my work, and my work has been killing people. It's the only thing that I'm good at. I mean, what reasons do I have to lead a decent life, anyway? My brain is messed up with this Isabella Carla thing. I dream of cows and grass almost every time I go to sleep. I only know how to chase, to hunt down, and to kill. Fuck. I'm a loser. I'm even too much of a loser to get myself killed, so I just kill everyone else instead. You're better off without me, Petra. I'm telling you now because if you stick around me, sooner or later you're going to get yourself taken out. Maybe even by me."

"I don't believe that," Petra sniffed. "I mean, I believe that you're crazy. And I believe that you're dangerous. But I don't believe that you would ever kill me. Not the same guy who cried in my office. Who carried me out of a kill zone at Nupierre. Who covered me with a blanket and held me because I was upset. Who let me point his gun at him, loaded and cocked, and trusted me not to pull the trigger. No. That guy would never kill me, even though he's only known me for one day. A full and scary day, but only one day."

"So I'm not so bad, then?" Jim probed.

"No," Petra shook her head and smiled sadly. "You're not so bad."

Jim was silent for a moment.

"Well, how about a shag, then?"

"Aaargh!" Petra screamed, and threw her hands up to the air. "You!"

Jim laughed, and settled back into his psychiatrist couch for a nap.

CHAPTER 6:
WHERE JIM GETS STUBBORN

When they got to Central City, Petra made a few calls and narrowed the field down to three stations: Central Broadcasting Co-op (CBC), Central Broadcasting Galaxy-Wide (CBGW), and Central Broadcasting Body (CBB). These were three of the wealthiest and most influential broadcasting organisations in the system, and that meant that they were three of the most influential organisations of anyone, anywhere. Full stop.

They tried CBC first, on a hunch of Jim's. Basically, it was closest to the spaceport.

The CBC building sat at the end of a massive, cobblestone square – Central Broadcasting Plaza, it was called. The building rose 75 storeys up, and its outside – including all doors and windows – was covered entirely in mirrored glass. As he got closer, Jim looked in the door to adjust his collar. The double doors slid open automatically for them, and slid automatically shut behind them. Instantly, Jim got a bad feeling.

The entire bottom floor was deserted. Not a sausage stirred anywhere across the shiny polished expanse. "I have a bad feeling about this," he said to Petra. "Where are all the people?"

All was still and silent.

Then a door opened on the far side of the room, and a man in a heavily armoured black suit, with a wall shield held out in front of him, walked into the room. There was no way Jim could hit him with a shot, not even a lucky one. A dozen more like him came out, and behind them came a dozen more, each armed with the latest and most powerful stun-slug weapons. The same thing happened at a door to his left, and again, at a door on his right. Jim pulled out his guns.

The sound of 75 rifles cocking simultaneously is bound to make anyone think of their own mortality. Even Jim Holloway. Jim turned to Petra with a grimace. "Seventy-five to one. I think we may have a problem here."

Petra pulled her gun out of its holster and – holding it gingerly, like it was some kind of big insect – she placed it on the ground in front them. She nodded for Jim to do the same. He did – slowly, and very reluctantly.

"Well done, Mr Holloway," a voice boomed over hidden speakers seemingly lining the room. From above the main entrance desk, a large screen – 15 foot wide by 20 foot long – slid out of the ceiling. Jim and Petra turned to the screen. It flickered to life, and a long, dark-haired, tanned-skinned, pale-eyed face stared down on them. "Well done indeed, Mr Holloway," the face said again. "It's impressive that you even made it here, and now that you have, that you have defied every instinct in your body that is practically screaming for you to shoot your way to a glorious and bloody death. You put your guns down as tamely and meekly as a lamb. Well done, Jim Holloway."

"Who the fuck are you?" Jim demanded.

"Oh, I do apologise," replied the face. "I am the man who has made you famous, Jim. Do you watch much TV, I wonder?"

Jim shook his head. "No."

"Ah well, that's a shame. There are over 400 system-wide TV channels, and this station owns almost a hundred of them. Across the 40 planets of this system, that means almost 50 billion people a day watch the programmes aired by this broadcasting station. And I," the face stated proudly, "am one of the best producers working for this station."

"What shows have you done?" Petra piped up.

"Why thank you for asking, little lady." The face smiled. "I've done *Zak is Back*, *Nimble Aunty*, and seven *Viewers' Choice* episodes, amongst others."

Petra was impressed. "Some good shows."

The face tried to look gracious, but failed. "Yes, well, one does try, sweet-cheeks. But my latest effort is by far the most popular I have ever done. Only three episodes into the programme, and already 55 channels have called up asking for it. It was a pilot project – a little scheme used to test the water. Gauge public opinion, so to speak. And it has been a resounding success."

Jim was beginning to get impatient. "What has this got to do with me?" he cut in. "Or Isabella Carla, for that matter?"

"Everything, Jim..." The face began to fade from the screen, and was replaced by a test pattern. "I think you should watch this," the voice continued. "I am Manny Dryer, and I am the producer of this show. We will talk again afterwards."

A title in bold orange flickered across the screen – *Guns and Broads* – only to be shot by an imaginary gun, and as the screen bled, the title shot faded away, to be replaced by the beautiful Linda Taratello, with a microphone in her hand.

"Welcome to episode 1 of *Guns and Broads*, the show that takes you into the violence and out onto the mean streets…"

*

As images of Jim's life over the past few days flashed across the screen above him, Jim thought about his current situation. Seventy-five to one were not good odds. But at the same time, they only had stun-slug rifles. Powerful weapons for stopping a man, yes. But for killing a man? No. They shot charged, rubberised projectiles which were programmed to release their charge as soon as they hit. This meant that they could virtually take a man out by hitting him almost anywhere on the body. Glancing blows aside, a direct hit almost anywhere would most likely render a person unconscious.

Jim looked briefly up at the screen. A panel of experts was critiquing his shooting of Johnny Centauri. The special forces representative, a Captain John Stryker, with a box cut and cop moustache, was commenting on how poor Jim's technique had been. Then, using the latest holographic video imaging, he replayed the killing the way he would have done it – from across the street with his limited-edition, high-powered, max-velocity Trema 10 rifle with uranium-depleted shells, a laser scope, three stun grenades, and a flashbang sense depressor. He would have crossed the gap between the buildings using a lightweight, reinforced cable coil on collapsible, double-headed concrete penetration arrows, shot into the side of Johnny's building with a computer-guided automatic wall penetration unit (AWPU).

After that, he would have slid into Johnny's apartment and peppered his body with three-by-three round bursts, just to make certain he was dead. And then, after spraying the room with random suppressive fire, he would have secured the perimeter.

Jim wondered why, if the captain had access to that much firepower, he didn't just nuke the whole, damn building, and pick the bodies out of the rubble. All in all, Jim thought, Captain John Stryker was an asshole.

Getting back to his current problem, though, Jim figured he could most likely make it to where he had put his guns on the floor before they got a shot off at him. It wasn't that Jim had any pressing urge to escape; he just couldn't handle the thought of these fucks playing him, getting away with it, and then making him surrender on top of it. Making him look like a fool; showing him no respect.

Suddenly, a metaphorical lightbulb went on in Jim's head.

Respect.

That was it. They didn't respect him. All he wanted was to be left alone, and they didn't respect that. Jim's anger rose. They would pay, he thought. They would pay dearly, because nobody messed with Jim Holloway and got away with it. THE Jim Holloway. Mr JP Holloway. The big Mr James. The meanest son of a bitch in Emera City, and beyond.

Jim could feel his temper reaching breaking point. The nearest cover was across the lobby, between the counterand the central column that housed the elevators. It was over 20 yards away. Almost 60 feet. He reckoned they would hit him with at least ten rounds before he got there. Jim wasn't so sure he could survive that. He began to get more irritable, and started tapping his foot. As he watched the commentary continue on the large screen, he rubbed his hands together. He bobbed his head. He hummed to himself.

Pressure built within him, slowly and surely, like a volcano of hate and lava beneath the surface of Jim's brain.

Petra turned to him and put a hand on his arm.

"Jim," she whispered urgently. "Calm down. These guys will kill you the first chance they get. Don't give them an excuse!"

In Jim's mind, he saw himself charging out of a wooden barn in the style of *Butch Cassidy and the Sundance Kid*, shooting up the marshals, going down in a blaze of glory. In the lobby, his whole body started to quiver. Onscreen, he was wading through a scene of carnage at the Nupierre Institute.

"Jim, no!" Petra shouted.

And that was all Jim needed.

"Yaaaah!" Jim screamed out of pure frustration, and dived forward for his guns. As he did so, the bass-like thump of stun-slug rifles being fired filled his ears. He rolled smoothly and collected his weapons in one movement. Behind him, Petra caught three rounds, and crumpled into a twitching heap. That made Jim even more angry.

He ran as fast as he could, one gun to the left, one to the right, empty shell casings flying into the air, shiny nozzles belching smoke, fire, and thunder.

It was an awe-inspiring sight. One of his bullets caught a soldier in the eye, and exploded his head like a grapefruit dropped from a four-storey building. Halfway across the room, Jim took a hit in the calf. His whole leg spasmed, and he almost fell, but somehow he forced his body on, willing it forward out of pure hate, rage, and frustration. En route to the counter, he took three more stun bullets: one in the arm, one in the chest, and one in the back. The last two hit him while he was in the air, stretched in full flight, diving over the counter into the small cover and relative safety behind it. He landed heavily on the cold, hard floor, his whole body spasming, racked with the jolt-like pain that the charges delivered. He fought the urge to scream.

Jim lay on the floor, unable to move, battling to hold onto consciousness. The veins at his temples throbbed and he clenched his jaw. Sweat poured down his blotchy forehead, mottled with patches of white and red, as his blood flow interrupted and pulsed in response to the heavy charges running through his body. He thought he was going to die.

Through the massive pounding of his heart in his ears, he could barely make out the sound of the soldiers on the other side radioing for backup and then preparing to move in and inspect for Jim behind the counter. They were doing it slowly, because with Jim, you could never be too sure.

Good, Jim thought to himself. Let them be scared. Then his body spasmed again. As Jim lay there, paralysed, battling against the bright starbursts in his head, with steel bands of pain squeezing his chest, he felt them begin to move in. Jim focused every ounce of strength in his body, every fibre of his being, on trying to move his gun.

It moved.

Jim howled out to the soldiers in pure defiance, too much hate flowing through him to even form words – not that his stiffened and clamped vocal cords were in any condition to make them anyway.

"Aaaaagh!" Jim screamed, and squeezed the trigger of his gun.

As the boom of its shot died down, Jim heard the sound of soldiers scattering for cover. Their voices echoed over the counter to Jim.

They couldn't believe that he was conscious. Or even alive. He had made it across the counter alive. And then he had stayed conscious. And then, he had even fired a shot. Every soldier claimed to have shot him – it was impossible, with so many hits, that he could have done what he did. Jim was an android, they said. He was a military experiment. Fuck all of that, Jim thought. He was just pissed off.

The prickle of sensation began to return to his left leg and right arm. They hadn't been hit. On the floor a few feet away from him lay the computer console that usually rested on the countertop. His nose was bleeding, badly. His head felt like it was being crushed in a vice. Through gritted teeth, Jim breathed harsh and ragged breaths, the taste of his own blood running out his nose and into his mouth.

They wanted tough, did they? Jim would show them tough. Dragging his body over towards the computer console took Jim almost two minutes. The minute he touched the keys, the computer screen lit up. Dripping blood and sweat onto the fancy keyboard, Jim punched in Manny Dryer's name. Instantaneously, the screen changed, and Manny's credentials and office suite typed in bright blue across the top of the screen. He was on the 27th floor, office 2717. Jim squeezed off another shot, just to scare the soldiers, and then began to drag his semi-paralysed body back though the slick of his own blood to the elevators.

*

"Please state your desired destination?"

"Twenty-seven." Jim mouthed out as best he could. He had to say it three times before the computer recognised what he said, and the doors shut, and the elevator swooshed smoothly upwards. His head swirling in a multicolour haze, Jim finally passed out.

And awoke with a bing.

The elevator had arrived. The doors opened onto an empty passageway that stretched out long and straight in front of him, with doors lining either side. He probably needed 15 or 20 minutes for the charges to wear off. He had maybe three to five before the soldiers downstairs gathered the courage to track him down. This time, he was sure, they would use real bullets.

Struggling to his feet, half leaning against the wall, Jim slid his mostly inert body down the lengthy passageway. He passed door 2701. Then 2703. There weren't many people in the passage, but those who were shrieked at the sight of him and ran back to lock themselves in their offices.

Finally, he approached door 2717. It was painted burgundy, with a gold handle and door frame. Manny Dryer's name was printed in gold across the top in large Times New Roman letters.

Jim knocked.

The door slid open to reveal a plush reception suite, manned by a beautiful and fresh-faced young secretary. Straightaway, she saw Jim.

"Oh shit!"

"Damn right, little lady," Jim slurred and raised his gun. "'Oh shit!' is right. Press any button, and you get a hole in your pretty forehead. Understand?"

She nodded and raised her hands in the air.

"Now, which one is Dryer's office?"

She nodded towards the middle door.

"You know who I am?"

She nodded.

"You know what happens if you mess with me?" he quizzed her.

She nodded again, and pressed the tip of her middle finger against her forehead.

"That's right," Jim drawled. "A hole right there. Now, if I were you, I'd leave quickly, because things are about to get ugly."

She turned and ran from the room, leaving Jim alone, facing Mannie Dryer's closed office door. He went over to the receptionist's desk and found the control console for the front door of the suite. He pressed the lock button and heard a satisfying click. That would keep the soldiers off his back for a few moments longer. Jim walked across the room and opened the door to the inner office.

"Frieda, I told you not to… Oh, shit!"

Jim grinned at Mandezo Dryer. "Yah, I seem to be getting that sort of reaction lately." He waved his gun at Manny, and motioned towards a wheelie chair in the corner near the window, overlooking the city. "Sit down."

Manny Dryer sat down. He was nervous. Sweat was forming on his face, and he repeatedly smoothed the wispy strands of hair that fell across the front of his forehead with soft, clammy hands.

"Jim, you don't understand. It was for the people. It's the future of television…"

"You messed with my head," Jim replied. "You fucked with my life. You had no right to do that."

"Ah, so what, Jim?" Manny stood up from his chair. "Your life was a heap of shit before I came along, anyway. Now you're famous." He motioned to a bank card lying on his desk. "Not to mention rich. The studio said I had to pay you royalties for the three episodes. It's attuned to your DNA; only you can collect."

"But…"

"Fuck it, Jim!" Manny brought the edge of his right hand down through the air and forcefully slammed it into the palm of his left. "Don't you get it? You had nothing, and I've given you everything! You're famous, you have more money than you have ever had in your life, and in the next room, I have something that you want more than anything else in the world."

Jim felt butterflies in his stomach. "Yes?"

"I have the woman of your dreams – Isabella Carla." Manny walked very slowly and cautiously over to his desk – he knew that any sudden movement could set Jim off, and he didn't want that. He had to survive until security arrived. At all costs, he had to survive.

Manny pressed the intercom button on his switchboard, and signalled the office next door. "Lynda, please bring Ms Carla here."

He took his finger off the button. A few seconds later, his office door opened, and Lynda Taratello walked in. Behind her, attired in a white dress and smelling of flowers, came Isabella Carla. Jim stumbled. He pressed a hand against the wall to keep himself up.

Manny sat on his desk.

Jim felt an uncontrollable need to rush over to Isabella Carla and hold her. He had to have her in his arms, where she belonged. In his mind's eye, he saw the two of them far away together, happy, on a farm somewhere, with children and warm, sunny skies.

"Jim!" Manny Dryer broke the spell.

Jim tore his gaze from the still-silent Isabella to face the skinny producer.

"What have you done to me?" he asked.

"What we have done to you is called Project Pandora,"

Manny answered proudly. "It started out as a top-secret galactic infiltration exercise on silent assassination, but died because of lack of funding. I – that is, CBC – took it up, and the result stands here before you today. Beautiful, isn't she?"

Jim nodded silently. She was indeed beautiful.

"You see," Manny went on. "Over the last ten years, the woman you know as Isabella Carla has been treated with a range of chemical additives to alter her fundamental biological composition. She is the same as you or me, except for the fact that she is a gene-spliced killing machine. To touch her is to die. Programmed within her very genetic makeup are the chemicals that are churning your brain into butter even as we speak. Other subjects who were exposed to Isabella's chemicals killed themselves in a matter of days. One, within four hours. You, though, Jim, are something special, I've got to give you that. You are one tough son of a bitch."

Jim had to agree. He *was* one tough son of a bitch. But now he had to break out of this madness. He had to get himself right, somehow. He asked Manny: "But how do I stop it?"

Manny's smile grew even wider. "That's not easy, I'm afraid. The chemicals are space-synapsed with basic residual core links to the host's body."

Jim was growing tired of Manny Dryer. He cocked his weapon and pointed it at the small man. "In English, Manny."

Manny stuttered nervously for a few seconds before getting it out. "The infecting virus will only die if the host dies."

"And that means..." said Jim, with a spreading feeling of dread.

"It means that the only way for your head to be right again is for you to kill the woman you dream about. The woman you can't live without."

Jim felt as if he'd been hit with a sledgehammer. He slumped against the wall and dropped his head to his chest. His guns fell to his sides. He wanted to give up.

And then Isabella Carla spoke.

"Jim, you wouldn't kill me, would you?" Her voice was exactly like he had imagined it would be. Feminine. Slightly throaty. Beautiful.

She took a step towards Jim, but stopped at a motion of Manny's hand. She raised her hands out to Jim. "Come to me, Jim. Hold me."

It was the most inviting thing Jim had ever heard said in his life. He lurched over to her and wrapped his arms around her. She felt so warm and soft – just as he'd dreamed. She smelt so good, he could just breathe her in forever. She lifted the bottom hem of her A-line dress and wiped some blood from his face. She smiled at him. Right then, he was the centre of the universe. He didn't give a damn about cows or grass or people or anything else. Not even himself. All he needed was a kiss. And to hold her in his arms until the sun fell down from the sky.

Jim and Isabella kissed.

And in the metallic gleam of Lynda Taratello's handbag, Jim saw Isabella's hand raise behind his back, holding a small, pointed knife.

Jim thrust Isabella away and leapt back against the wall. Her knife cut through the air only inches from his face.

She was still smiling at him.

"I told you, Jim," said Manny. "She is truly beautiful. A beautiful killing machine. And she kills whomever I need her to – and right now, that is you."

Manny ducked behind the desk as Jim shot at him. The bullet punched a fat, round hole in the glass pane behind the desk, sailing over the city.

Then Jim did the hardest thing he had ever had to do in his life. He killed Isabella Carla. He pumped three bullets into her beautiful, sun-kissed body: one in her throat, one in her chest, and one in her right shoulder. She fell to the ground, her white dress splattered with blood. Her face wore an expression of devastation. Jim had betrayed her.

Her eyes rolled back in her head as the blood drained out of her, and she fell to the floor, dead.

For a split-second, Jim felt as if his heart had been ripped out of his chest and torn in two by a giant bird with unimaginably sharp claws. He stopped breathing. The shock of its host virus dying sent the virus in Jim's mind into an epileptic death throe. Jim wailed, incomprehensible and agonisingly sad. In that one moment, every sadness, every hate, every hurt, pain, anger, and loss tore their way out of his throat and into the air. Jim screamed for at least a minute, before his throat was too raw to continue.

The silence after the scream was heavy with sorrow. And regret. And grief. Now the only noise in the room was the ragged sound of Jim's heavy breathing.

He had never felt this way before. Or if he had, it had been such a long time ago that he had forgotten what it felt like.

Strangely, though, he felt light. Tired, bruised, battered, and sore. Emotionally exposed and tender. But also light. Finally, he had shaken off the baggage he had been carrying ever since Marge had left.

Looking up, Jim realised that Lynda Taratello had run out of the room in terror. He didn't blame her. He was, after all, a pretty terrifying guy. He did terrifying things.

Jim moved behind the desk and dragged out a quivering and petrified Manny Dryer.

"If you want to live, call your soldiers off," he told him.

Manny scrambled for the intercom and hurriedly gave the command.

"Good," said Jim. "Now, pass me that bank card."

Manny did so.

"And your Rolex. I also want your Rolex."

"But…"

"Give it." Jim cut him short.

Manny pulled his favourite Rolex from his vein-riddled wrist, and dropped it in Jim's hand.

"And now," said Jim. "Goodbye."

Jim shot Manny Dryer in the head. Once. Between the eyes. At close range. Manny's dead body slumped to the floor.

Jim slipped the bank card and the watch into his pocket, and limped slowly out of the room.

*

Senator Hymes stood over Manny Dryer's body. Across the desk, General Abhakar and Special Agent Chief Simione stood closely together, waiting for the senator to continue.

"And so, after watching the footage on the security tapes, I get the distinct impression that our TV producer over here got exactly what he was looking for. He wanted death and mayhem, and he got death and mayhem…" He waved the cassette in his hand. "All recorded on TV."

"And Jim Holloway?" asked Simione.

"Oh, I don't know," replied the senator. "I don't think we'll be seeing much of him for a very long time."

Abhakar nodded, his walrus moustache bobbing. "I

concur, senator. He always wanted to be left alone. Now he has enough money to be able to do just that."

Reluctantly, Simione agreed. "Yes, I suppose you are right. But what about the missing agent?"

"I suspect," smiled Hymes, "that she is not 'missing', and is very happy where she is right now. Wherever that may be."

"But…"

The senator raised a hand to cut Simione off. "But nothing, Simione. Those two have been through enough. And for what? Entertainment? No, not on my watch. Not in my town. They will be left alone – by every one of the departments under my jurisdiction. Is that clear?"

Simione nodded grudgingly.

Senator Hymes tossed the cassette in his hand to General Abhakar.

"General, after reviewing the evidence, I find Jim Holloway not guilty of all crimes, acquitted on grounds of maliciously induced insanity. I also discharge Petra Verkayik from any contractual obligations she has towards any of our municipal departments."

The general smiled and nodded. "Yes, sir."

"Good. Then the case is closed." The senator stepped out from behind the desk to leave the room. In his way to the door, he stopped and turned to Simione.

"Oh, by the way, Simione, come with me. I have some gentlemen downstairs from central office who are interested in your financial dealings with the networks." The senator beamed his biggest grin at the agent.

Simione paled visibly.

*

The sun shone yellow, beautiful and proud. Jim felt glad to be alive. He walked back out into his front yard and stretched. Before him, the half-painted white picket fence gleamed as the morning sun caught the still-wet glistening drips of paint. Beyond that, a handful of cows mooed and cudded cheerfully to themselves in the field that Jim owned. Behind him was his double-storey house, and to the left was his barn. His red tractor waited in the barn.

To his right, a panoramic view greeted him: green hill after green hill, criss-crossed with a patchwork of farmlands and wooded groves, browns and yellows, light and dark greens in a truly ordered pandemonium – the kind that only Mother Nature at her best could provide. The smell of sizzling bacon wafting out of his house reminded Jim that he was hungry – his lady was in the kitchen, cooking breakfast.

"Don't be long, Jim," she called. "Breakfast is almost ready."

Jim smiled before he answered, just appreciating for a moment how good life could actually be.

"Don't worry, Petra," he called back. "I'll be there right now."

And somewhere in Jim's head, a cow mooed.

Fin.

BOOKS BY THIS AUTHOR

Bad Medicine

Eddie Burma is the wizard that people come to when they have a problem…but what happens when the problems come looking for him?

After seeing an old acquaintance murdered, Eddie lands back in his quiet hometown, only to end up in conflict with a criminal coven he thought was long gone.

He also needs to deal with an ancient spirit that has re-appeared after hundreds of years, the assassination attempts by magically enhanced hit teams, and the demon possessed bikers. Then he still needs to get to the undead evil behind it all. Meanwhile, the bodies keep piling up.

Amidst the chaos, he somehow needs to train up his new apprentice; a 16-year-old girl with far too much moxy and talent for her own good.

Finally, when Eddie's problems take the shape of a terrifying, soul-sucking shaman, he has to put everything on the line in a desperate fight to keep himself and his loved ones alive.

Welcome to the first book in your new favorite Urban Fantasy series. If you're a Jim Butcher, Shayne Silvers and Michael Anderle fan, then this fast-paced, action-packed, magical series is for you.

Court Of Fey

An Ancient elven court steeped in intrigue. Mythic assassins carry-out slaughter wholesale. A demon lord chews through victims like a quarterback on painkillers, and all the while a sinister organisation of twisted mages seek to further their unspeakable agenda.

When Eddie and the Family are called to the Autumn kingdom to help in an ancient Elven rite, they cross the Winter Fey, and Eddie ends up fighting to survive against an undead dark elf, frost giants, assassins and trolls.

If that's not enough, the family finally track down Bethshiel, the fleeing Demon lord, and they corner him into a showdown that they're not sure they can win.

Dark secrets come to light and past collides with present as Eddie and the family power through byzantine intrigue and reckless danger. As the stakes get ever bigger they are faced with the possibility that they just might not make it out alive.

Court of Fey is the second instalment in the Rules of Magic, Urban fantasy series. If you like intense action, fantastic magic and relatable characters then you won't want to put this series down!

BONUS CONTENT: LISTEN TO THE CAT...

You are having a nightmare. Your arms are rigid at your side, and you cannot move your legs. It feels as if your entire body is cocooned in immovable bands of steel, and with a great effort, you open your eyes.

You see that you are floating, drifting down a grey steel passageway, slowly, but precisely, towards a faint light at the far end.

Now it comes back to you – you had fallen asleep on the couch, reading – and had suddenly woken up as some unseen force, some giant telekinetic hand lifted you off the couch, and out the window. Terror built inside of you... fear, anger, and instantly, you had passed out again as though a switch had been flipped off.

Now, awake, the nightmare continues. You find yourself well and truly restrained, floating down a passageway towards a door with a small oval window, out of which, streams a faint, white light.

You realise that it is cold, and you are paralysed from below your neck, and are floating face down and naked. Frustratingly, and adding to the terror, you cannot utter a sound.

The door gently slides open with a shushing sound and in the room before you is a scene to terrify the most steadfast of hearts.

A grey alien, thin limbed with a pear-shaped,wrinkled body, an oval head dominated by two large, bulbous, glass-gem eyes the size of apples, stands next to a bed and a tall shining machine of mechanical arms, blades, and probes.

It dawns upon you then, that you are naked, backside in the air, and are drifting unopposed to an alien and his probe machine. The smile on the aliens face widens as you approach, and the telekinetic force that propelled you down the passageway, now rests you on the hard, steel bed, and holds you down. The door shushes to a close behind you.

You turn your head, and the alien positively leers at you.

"Hello, human." His voice intrudes upon your mind.

"My name will not translate well into your primitive brain, so it is best that you call me Rete. I am a Keleppian, and I will be probing you today."

He moves to the machine, briefly out of sight.

"Probing you gives me no pleasure." His voice slides into

your mind from behind the machine, which begins to buzz and show signs of life.

"But there is a certain satisfaction in a job well done, you understand. I merely take joy in fulfilling my duty…"

The door slides open. "Oh really?" A second voice sounds in your mind. This one is proud and raspy. It isn't cold, like the alien's, but somehow, feels warm and satisfying. Like milk at bedtime.

It is the voice of a cat. Standing in the entranceway, you see a black cat, with white mittens and a white patch above his right eye. Flecks of gold sparkle in his eyes, and he has about him an air of rogue like danger.

"Rete the Keleppian and human probe subject; I am Tammit Swishtail, Lord of Bowls." His tail gently swishes behind him, and he bows his head in greeting.

You still cannot move your body or speak, but you do nod your head as best you can. Rete, the Keleppian alien goes rigid. Although alien, it seems that fear shows the same body language across all races in the galaxy. It is clear that the alien fears the cat.

"Lord Tammit," the cold, steely voice of the alien rings in your head. "I had not known you were in these precincts." He pauses. "I was merely gathering samples, this human volunteered for a brief swab test." He runs a small swab of fabric along your calf.

"There. All done! See? No harm, no foul, as it is said on this planet."

He puts the swab in a chute on the side of the machine.

The telekinetic hand lifts you up off the bed, and places you on your feet, and the pressure eases off you. You lean, groggily, and unsteadily against the steel bed.

"Alien, we will continue this discussion later." The cat's voice sounds firm, in your mind. "If you try run for it, I will be speaking with your superiors."

Rete's grey face pales to a dirty white. He clasps his long-fingered hands in front of his abdomen and bows his head. "That will not be necessary, Lord of bowls."

Tammit stands up, and in the slow sauntering way that cats have, he walks over to you and gently rubs up against your leg.

"We shall see, what will, or will not be necessary, alien." he says.

Then, he sits at your feet, and looks up towards you.

"Human – you have just read the Science fiction story, TV future? The book of the author Horsman, yes?"

Still numb, you nod your head.

"Good. Now you must leave a review and must tell others how it was exceedingly entertaining. It's good that you share this joy with them, yes?"

You nod again, like a tired child taking notes from a schoolteacher.

"Also, you must join his newsletter. He actually won't send you a letter of news, it will be an electronic mail – an email once a week. I have been told that it provides such delight as humans cannot hope to contain."

"Aah, pardon me." Rete the Keleppian piped up.

"Would author Horsman mind if aliens joined his electronic mail of news?"

Tammit turns his head sideways in thought.

"That would be suitable." He says after a while. "Author Horsman is friend to all. Cat and creature, bug and beast. Human and alien. Even," a small sigh, "the dog."

"Scan the code below to join the newsletter." The cat stands up and prepares to leave.

He looks at the alien. "There will be no more probing, understand?"

Before the alien answers, he turns to face you.

"Review, and newsletter – don't forget!"

Then he proceeds to sashay in that slow and swaying walk that cats have, out of the room.

Your eyes grow heavy, and they slide shut, like the door on an alien spaceship. As you fall asleep again, somehow with the feeling of your couch, warm beneath you, the words of Lord Tammit sit fixed in your mind.

"Review, and newsletter – don't forget!"